PRAISE FOR IRIS MORLAND

PETAL PLUCKER

Funny, charming, and utterly captivating! I devoured this sparkling read.

— ANNIKA MARTIN, NEW YORK TIMES
BESTSELLING AUTHOR

Petal Plucker was funny, entertaining, fresh and fan-yourself-worthy . . . Their enemies-to-lovers romance is both charming, tender and steamy, and you'll love both of these characters (and their families!) and their sigh-worthy happily ever after.

— MARY DUBÉ, CONTEMPORARILY EVER
AFTER

Morland has created a masterpiece of a romance . . . one of my favorite [books] of the year.

— CRISTIINA READS

Humorous, raunchy, and refreshing, Petal Plucker has rightfully earned its way, in my opinion, as one of the best romantic comedy [books] this year.

— CAROL, TIL THE LAST PAGE

My One and Only

This book was gripping, well written & the chemistry between the characters sizzled throughout this wonderful read.

— AMAZON REVIEW

All I Want Is You

Another heartfelt, steamy, terrific story. This is an author who really knows how to create a story that catches a reader's attention and characters that capture her heart.

— BOOKADDICT

TAKING A CHANCE ON LOVE

Thea and Anthony are in for a surprise when it comes to the language of the heart . . . I am in awe.

— HOPELESS ROMANTIC BLOG

Then Came You

This story really pulled all my heartstrings. This was truly a beautiful story and makes you believe there really is true love out there.

— MEME CHANELL BOOK CORNER

ALSO BY IRIS MORLAND

ROMANTIC COMEDIES

He Loves Me, He Loves Me Not

Petal Plucker

War of the roses

LOVE EVERLASTING

including

THE YOUNGERS

Then Came You

Taking a Chance on Love

All I Want Is You

My One and Only

THE THORNTONS

The Nearness of You

The Very Thought of You

If I Can't Have You

Dream a Little Dream of Me

Someone to Watch Over Me

Till There Was You

I'll Be Home for Christmas

HERON'S LANDING

Seduce Me Sweetly

Tempt Me Tenderly

Desire Me Dearly

Adore Me Ardently

THE VERY THOUGHT OF YOU

THE THORNTONS

IRIS MORLAND

BLUE VIOLET PRESS LLC

For everyone who loved Harrison and Sara's story and wanted more.
Thank you!

THE VERY THOUGHT OF YOU

"You gonna do something with that loaf of bread, or are you just going to stare at it until it bursts into flames?"

Megan Flannigan looked up from the burnt loaf of banana bread currently sitting on her bakery's counter to gaze into the green eyes of her greatest nemesis, Caleb Thornton. Her heart fluttered into her throat, which annoyed her beyond anything.

"I was just thinking," she retorted. "Until you interrupted me."

"Now I'm curious what you were thinking about with that frown on your face."

She opened her mouth, but closed it just as quickly. Her injured hand—cut a week prior on one of the many kitchen knives in her bakery—tingled. Or maybe it merely ached. She wasn't sure how to parse her feelings about much of anything anymore.

Caleb Thornton never failed to rouse both her irritation and her desire in equal measures. With his careless good looks, green eyes, and angelic grin, he could get the devil himself to do what he wanted with his charm. Couple that with his police uniform, and he was a veritable bombshell of masculine attraction.

Which was the precise reason why Megan really, really hated him.

"That's none of your business," she replied primly. Taking the burnt banana bread, she tossed it into the trash with a sigh. At his raised eyebrows, she explained, "My timer broke, and I didn't realize it until I'd burnt the loaf."

"It didn't look that burned."

"Believe me, you wouldn't want to eat it. I can't serve that to my customers, anyway."

Megan had opened her bakery, The Rise and Shine, a year ago, and although she was hardly an expert in running a small business, she'd managed to attain enough success that she wasn't afraid that she'd have to close her doors. After working at odd jobs here and there in her early twenties, she'd made the terrifying decision to quit her most-hated office job to start her bakery. She'd begun baking only a few years prior, and she'd discovered that she loved it.

"Can I get you something? Or are you just here to lurk?" she asked.

Caleb barked a laugh. "How's your hand?" When she'd cut it, he'd been with her, and he'd bandaged it himself.

Megan could still feel his fingers against her palm, warm and rough and gentle.

She showed him her hand, which was healing nicely. "It's fine. No stitches needed. Although I've made sure to keep any knives from sitting in the sink. I'd rather not have a repeat incident."

"That's probably a good idea."

Megan realized with an indrawn breath that they were alone in the bakery. Again. Caleb's younger sister and Megan's one employee, Jubilee Thornton, was running an errand. It was the hour before school was let out, so Megan's usual parents and kids that came in for an afternoon snack hadn't arrived yet.

How did she always end up alone with Caleb?

"I'd recommend the carrot cake," she said, to answer a question he hadn't asked. She reached inside the case and began to place a piece on a plate. "This version doesn't have raisins. I think more people hate raisins than like them." She knew she was babbling. She clapped her mouth shut, trying not to blush.

He took the proffered cake. "I agree. Raisins are the worst." He picked up a fork and began to eat the cake. When he groaned out loud, it sent shivers down Megan's spine.

"You do have to pay for that."

He reached into his back pocket and handed her a five-dollar bill. "That cover it?"

"Good enough." She finished the transaction and said in a brisk voice, "I need to start up another loaf of banana bread before the afternoon rush. Do you need anything else?"

"No, ma'am. I'm good with my cake right now."

Megan went to the back to start a second batch of banana bread. If another customer came in, she'd hear the front door bell jingle. Or Caleb would yell for her. She rolled her eyes. Caleb was like an annoying skin disease: no matter how hard she tried, she could not get rid of him.

She couldn't stop the smile from crossing her face at the idea of him as a skin disease. He'd love hearing that from her. As she grabbed the various ingredients for her bread, she entered into a kind of haze of baking: she was all hands and movements, her thoughts dissipating for a few blessed moments. The Caleb Thorntons of the world wouldn't bother her right now.

She heard footsteps right as she was about to turn on her mixer.

"Why are you back here?" she asked Caleb. "You know you don't work here, right?"

"And why are you always so annoyed to see me?"

She did not want to have this conversation. If he didn't know why she hated him, that was his problem, not hers. She turned her mixer on, effectively drowning out his voice.

He said something next to her, but she couldn't hear it. She shook her head and yelled, "I can't hear you!"

"I said I think we should call a truce!" he shouted.

She stopped the mixer. The silence stretched between them. "What?"

"I think we should call a truce. Aren't you tired of all of this?" He shrugged when she just stared. "I know you hate me or something, but I think it's time to set it aside. Water under the bridge and all that."

"Maybe for you," she said acidly. "It's easy to say it's all water under the bridge when you were the one who broke the bridge in the first place."

"Is that what that phrase is referencing?"

"Don't change the subject. You know exactly what I mean." She turned on the mixer again, her thoughts in disarray. Caleb Thornton represented so many things to her: disappointment, shame, resentment. Desire. Longing. *Insanity*.

When she turned off the mixer and began pouring the batter into a bread tin, Caleb said, "Look, I've asked you this before: is this about what happened ten years ago? When I arrested you?"

She whirled. Batter splattered onto the counter; she swore. "I am not having this conversation."

"You never want to have any conversation, Megan."

She refused to go back to that night. That stupid, stupid night, when she'd humiliated herself, and Caleb had been witness to it. When she looked into his eyes, she wondered if he thought about that night as much as she did.

"It's everything that's happened between us. Something happens, and then you push me away." She bit her tongue, unwilling to admit how much he'd hurt her.

But despite what she wanted to believe about him, Caleb managed to be more perceptive than she gave him credit. "Megan..." he said softly.

She held up a hand. "I don't want to have this conversation. I'm never going to be your biggest fan. Just get over it. I have."

What a liar, she thought.

She saw a tic in his jaw begin, and she knew he was getting frustrated with her. He always did.

"Considering your inability to have a conversation with me that doesn't involve sniping at me——"

"Because you always insult me!"

"When have I insulted you? Tell me. Because I sure as hell can't remember."

She opened the oven door and put the banana bread inside, the door closing with a slam. "If you can't figure it out, then I can't help you."

He groaned. "You are the most aggravating woman!"

"And you get on my nerves! Please leave. I have a business

to run, in case you forgot."

Opening his mouth to retort, Caleb seemed to think better of it. And luckily for the both of them, Jubilee came into the kitchen with bags of ingredients.

"They didn't have the usual brand of butter that you like—oh, Caleb. What are you doing here?" Jubilee asked.

With her dark hair and green eyes, Jubilee looked so much like Caleb that sometimes Megan had a hard time being around the girl. But unlike her brother, Jubilee was cheerful and helpful, and Megan had enjoyed getting to know her. Jubilee had been sheltered for most of her life, especially after multiple bouts with childhood cancer, and she'd only recently moved out of her parents' house and begun supporting herself. The newly added independence had only allowed her naturally sunny personality to shine through.

"I was just going, actually." Caleb turned to go before saying, "I'll see you later, Jubi."

The two women watched Caleb stalk out, not saying anything. Megan began to wash dishes, hoping that Jubilee wouldn't ask questions.

As usual, Megan's hopes were never meant to be.

"What was that about? He looked pissed. Why is it that every time you two are together, my brother gets angry and you get…well, just as angry?"

Megan scrubbed a pan with a special kind of vigor. "Your brother is an annoying asshole, and he gets on my nerves. That's all. Did you get brown sugar?"

"Don't change the subject." Jubilee pointed a spoon at her. "Tell me what's going on, or I'm going to get it out of my brother instead."

Megan chewed on the inside of her cheek. Part of her

wanted to confide in someone, but the other part of her knew very well that saying anything to Caleb's little sister would be bad news. Megan hadn't even told her own sister, Sara, about everything between her and Caleb.

She shrugged. "Nothing. We just don't get along."

"And I was born yesterday."

Jubilee began to put things away while Megan washed dishes. She didn't say anything for a few moments, and Megan almost breathed a sigh of relief that she'd decided to drop the subject.

"You know, it's funny," Jubilee remarked, "Caleb is probably the most easy-going of my brothers. Except maybe Harrison, although since he's the oldest, he's had his share of responsibilities. Caleb was my favorite as a kid, though. He would play games with me and bring me coloring books when I was in the hospital during treatments." Jubilee tossed the shopping bags into the catch-all bin for bags. "So what I'm trying to say is that he isn't the type of guy to get riled that easily. Unless it's about people dressing their pets in Halloween costumes. He really hates that."

Megan stopped washing dishes. Closing her eyes, she saw in her mind's eye two incidents, almost a decade apart. She thought of touches and kisses and desires concealed and unleashed, and she wondered if she would ever get them out of what felt like the very fiber of her being.

She didn't know how to respond to Jubilee's question. To her relief, she heard the front door bell jingle, signaling customers.

"Can you go get that?" she asked Jubilee. "This banana bread will be done soon, and I need to work on inventory."

"Okay, but don't think this is over. You don't know how

stubborn I can be." Jubilee smiled then, which made Megan smile as well. "Okay, maybe you can. You've known my family for long enough."

After Jubilee left to take care of the customers, Megan sat on a stool and waited for her banana bread to finish. *I do know how stubborn you Thorntons can be,* she thought, *and it's been the bane of my existence for longer than anyone realizes.*

MEGAN DIDN'T SLEEP that night. She dreamed of Caleb, and she couldn't get the heated image out of her brain no matter how hard she tried. Tired and grumpy, she got to the bakery an hour later than usual. She yawned as she approached the store. Then she stopped in her tracks when she saw the shattered glass covering the pavement.

She rushed toward the storefront. Gasping, she saw that one of the windows had been broken, and stepping over the broken glass carefully so she could unlock the front door, she took in the damage.

Chairs and tables had been scattered, while the cash register had been ransacked for cash. A few baked goods that had been left in the case over night had been tossed, and frosting and crumbs and sugar covered the floor and counters.

Her heart beating fast, Megan made her way to the back. The kitchen was worse off then the bakery: bags of flour and sugar had been dumped, while cartons of eggs had been smashed. She stood there and drank it all in, barely able to comprehend what she was seeing.

The safe. Had they found the safe?

She rushed to the tiny office adjacent to the kitchen,

unlocking the door with shaking fingers. She had always instructed Jubilee to keep any remaining cash in the safe when she closed up. She rushed inside to see the safe on its side and the back of it dented. After multiple tries to open it—her hands were shaking too badly to input the numbers correctly—she saw a stack of cash, checks and receipts inside.

She let out a breath of relief. Although there wasn't a ton of cash inside, it would've been a difficult loss to recoup at any rate. Megan closed the door of the safe and stood up, only to grab at the desk to steady herself. Her body wasn't working like it should. She realized, only slightly aware of herself, that she was probably in shock.

She barely remembered calling the cops. She'd known there was a good chance that Caleb would show up, and as she sat outside, staring at the rainbow of shattered glass on the pavement, she almost wished he would be the one on duty. He'd distract her. He'd annoy her so much that she wouldn't think about how someone had deliberately come inside her store and ripped it apart like some human tornado.

Tears threatened, hot and humiliating. She choked back a sob. She couldn't break down right now. Not before she could get home and be alone in her grief.

She considered calling Sara, but what could her sister do? Besides, Sara had done enough for Megan throughout her life. She'd practically raised her when their mother Ruth had been deep in her alcoholism, and Megan had tried not to rely on Sara so much. She could take care of herself.

She heard the sirens, and then she heard a voice asking, "Megan? Are you all right?"

Looking up, she gazed into the green eyes of Caleb Thornton. For the first time, she felt only relief at seeing him.

When Caleb had gotten the call from dispatch that there'd been a robbery at The Rise and Shine, he didn't consider why he'd driven like a madman to get there, or why the thought of Megan hurt and scared—had she been there when the robbery had occurred?—sent his thoughts into a tailspin.

He'd had to force his thoughts into the neat box of a police officer, not a concerned citizen. He had to exude calm and capability, even if everyone around him panicked.

It was easier said than done when he walked up to the bakery to see Megan sitting on a bench outside, looking as lost as when he'd arrested her.

"Megan, are you all right?"

He squatted down in front of her. He almost took her hands, but he wasn't Caleb Thornton right now: he was Officer Thornton, and he needed to keep a professional distance from this woman. No matter how much it tore him up inside to do so.

She glanced up. Her eyes were wide, bright blue, and he

was surprised to see that she wasn't crying. She just looked shocked.

"Caleb…" She blinked. "What…? Oh. Yes. There was a burglary."

He glanced at the shattered glass winking on the sidewalk, the broken window, and he could just make out the torn-up bakery inside. "Are you okay?" he asked in a firm voice. "Were you here when it happened? Should I take you to the hospital?"

When she didn't respond, he touched her shoulder. "Megan."

Her eyes widened. "No, no, I wasn't here. I got here this morning and this was what it looked like." She looked to see his hand resting on her arm.

He took his hand back and stood.

"Officer Gonzalez will be here to assist me. Do you want me to call anyone? Your sister?"

"No. Not yet." She bent down and was about to start picking up the pieces of glass, but Caleb stopped her.

"We need to take photos of the crime first," he explained gently. "And you don't want to cut yourself. How about you go across the street to the Fainting Goat and get something to eat? I know they're not open yet, but Trent will let us in—"

She stared at the ground, but after a moment, she shook herself. She rose, and Caleb was relieved to see a bit of color return to her face. "I'm not hungry. What can I do to help?"

There wasn't a whole lot beyond cataloguing what had been taken, since she hadn't been here to witness anything, but Caleb wasn't about to tell her that. Officer Juan Gonzalez, a middle-aged man who'd been on the force for twenty years, got out of his car and whistled at the damage. With his large, dark mustache and short stature, people had a tendency to underestimate him—until they saw how fast he could run, and how he could bench-press as much as any guy twice his height.

"Ms. Flannigan," Gonzalez said, "I'm sorry this has happened. Officer Thornton and I will be taking photos of the crime scene. Can you show us all the damage that you've noticed? And note anything missing?"

Megan seemed to come back to herself with something definite to do. Gonzalez escorted her inside, a fatherly air about him that usually calmed most people, with Caleb following behind.

Caleb's mind went into what he liked to term Officer Mode. There had been two other robberies in the neighborhood lately, although Megan's bakery had been the hardest hit, unfortunately. He grimaced as he took in the damage: the food scattered everywhere, the tipped-over and broken furniture, and the kitchen covered in flour and sugar and God knew what else. His boots crunched on glass, and he was glad to see that Megan wore thick shoes as well. If she'd been wearing her usual sandals, he wouldn't have let her in here.

As if she would've let me keep her out, he thought wryly. Megan Flannigan had never had any interest in listening to what he had to say.

"Was anything stolen?" Gonzalez asked. "Money? Equipment?"

Megan frowned. "I didn't see anything obvious stolen, but I haven't gone through the entire kitchen yet. They tried to get into the safe I keep in my office, but they weren't able to open it."

"Anything in the cash register?" Caleb asked.

"No, I don't keep money in the register over night, although Jubilee closed up last night. I need to call her…" Her voice trailed off as she gazed at a large smear of frosting on the display case. "Why would someone throw food around like this?"

"Megan—Ms. Flannigan," Caleb said in a low voice, "is there anyone you think might have a grudge against you? Any enemies you believe would do something like this?"

She let out a startled laugh. "Enemies? No, not really. Well," and her voice turned wry here, "only one, but I'm not sure he's much for robbing bakeries."

Caleb couldn't stop his lips from quirking into a grin. When Gonzalez gave him a curious look, he flattened his lips into a neutral expression. "I see. How about you call Jubi to come down so we can talk to her, and anyone else you think might know something. Gonzalez, you have your camera, right?"

"Let me go get it." Gonzalez looked at the pair of them but didn't say anything else.

Standing in the middle of the bakery, the chaos of the robbery all around them, Caleb couldn't help but think that Megan seemed so small amidst it all. Fragile, almost. He'd never in his life thought the words *fragile* and *Megan* in the same sentence, but there was a first time for everything.

"Hey, how are you holding up?"

She rubbed her arms before shrugging. "Fine. I mean, I'm not fine. I'm shocked, although I'm getting close to becoming angry. That's good, right?"

"I'd prefer to see an angry Megan than a quiet one, I'll admit."

Her rose-bud lips turned into a small smile. "I'd have to

agree. I don't like feeling like this. Like I'm out of control..." She shrugged again. "Which is ironic, if you think about it."

He wanted to take her into his arms. It was a ridiculous impulse: she'd never shown anything but antipathy toward him, yet he had this feeling, in the deepest part of him, that her thorns merely protected a soft, vulnerable center. Right now, he caught more glimpses of that vulnerability than he had in years, and he wanted to protect her. To enfold her in his arms and tell her she didn't have to be afraid, because he would keep her safe.

She blinked her blue eyes, her lashes sinfully long and dark. He watched as a slight flush rose on her cheeks. He opened his mouth to say something, anything, but Gonzalez took that moment to return.

"Sorry, the camera was buried underneath my son's soccer gear in the trunk. Caleb, let's get started?"

Caleb tore his gaze from Megan, although it was a struggle. He and Gonzalez canvassed the entire bakery, taking photos of all of the damage. As more and more of the thief's crime was revealed, he couldn't stop a black anger from taking hold of his insides. Only the lowest of assholes would do this to a woman who'd worked so hard to get this bakery started and make it successful. He wanted to find the guy—or woman—and wring his neck. Make him apologize to Megan and clean up every bit of flour and every cracked egg and every piece of broken glass until The Rise and Shine did, in fact, shine again.

"Do you think this is the same person who committed the other recent robberies?" Caleb asked quietly. It would make the most sense, although the other two robberies hadn't been nearly as destructive.

Gonzalez snapped a photo of an overturned vase of utensils. "Most likely. How many burglars are there in Fair Haven? Although it doesn't seem like he actually stole anything of value. He just wanted to destroy things." He frowned in thought. "That's honestly more concerning than somebody stealing money."

Caleb had to agree. This seemed to speak of some kind of grudge. Although Megan didn't think she had any enemies, he wondered now. Perhaps someone connected to the Flannigans who wanted to hurt them? He needed to talk to Harrison, although he might just be overly paranoid. The thief had tried to steal money from the safe. He might have realized his failure on that score and taken it out on the bakery as a result.

They both heard the front door bell ring, and then Caleb heard someone gasp behind him. "Oh my God! When Megan said we'd been robbed, I thought maybe they'd stolen some cash from the register..."

He turned to see his little sister Jubilee standing in the doorway of the kitchen. He smiled grimly at her. "Hey Jubi."

"This is terrible." She didn't even look at Caleb. "Poor Megan." She brushed a finger in some flour that had been thrown across a counter. "How are we going to clean all of this up?"

"You won't have to do it by yourselves." When Jubilee raised her eyebrows at Caleb's statement, he added gruffly, "Don't give me that look."

"What look? Am I looking at you somehow? Oh, hey, Juan. How are you? How's Gretchen and the kids?"

Gonzalez smiled. "They're great. Thanks for asking. Although you know my Joaquin? He twisted his ankle after the latest game and is out for the season. He's not too happy about it."

"That sucks. I'm sorry." Jubilee began to pepper Gonzalez with questions, which Caleb couldn't help but be grateful for. His little sister was better with people than he was, he thought wryly. Maybe she should have become a public servant instead of him.

"Do you think this person picked the bakery for a reason?" he heard Jubilee ask. "Or do you think it's random?"

"We don't have enough to go by right now, but given the extent of the damage, it's hard to think this was random," Gonzalez admitted. "Do you have any idea who could've done this? Somebody who's come in and gotten upset?"

She frowned. "I mean, beyond Mrs. Patterson getting mad when I accidentally put cream in her coffee? Not that I can think of. Mrs. Patterson is a bit touchy, but I don't think she'd break a window in revenge."

Gonzalez laughed. "I won't tell her you said that."

The front door bell rang again, and when Caleb, Gonzalez, and Jubilee stepped out of the kitchen into the bakery, Caleb saw Harrison and Sara entering, shocked expressions on their faces. Harrison, Caleb's older brother, had gotten engaged to Sara Flannigan—Megan's older sister—only a few weeks prior. Caleb couldn't help but notice the way his brother kept a hand on Sara's lower back, like he could shield her from the destruction around her. Harrison and Caleb looked alike, although where Harrison was broad, Caleb was taller. They both had the Thornton green eyes and dark hair. Sara and Megan, though, didn't look as much like sisters, although Caleb had noticed that they both shared similar expressions and mannerisms that marked them as related, if you paid attention. Sara was shorter and curvier with darker hair, whereas Megan was taller with deep red hair.

"Oh, Megan, this is awful." Sara glanced around. "I'm so sorry. Are you okay? Please tell me you weren't here when this happened. Why didn't you call earlier?"

Megan took her sister's hands. "Because I was dealing with the police, and besides, there wasn't anything you could do right then."

"I could've been with you!"

Megan looked like she wanted to argue that, but Harrison intervened smoothly, "Caleb, are you guys done so we can start cleaning up? Or do you need to take more photos?"

Gonzalez said, "We're done with photos. We'll be taking statements from here on. Caleb, how about you go talk the tenants next door, see if they saw anything. Megan and Jubilee, I'll take your statements, if you please."

Caleb wanted to argue—the last thing he wanted to do was leave Megan here—but he knew she had the support of her sister and his own siblings. As he walked out, though, he touched Megan's elbow, drawing her away from the circle.

"I'll be right next door if you need me."

When she didn't make her usual sassy remark, but instead just nodded, his chest tightened. He touched her arm once more before he stepped outside into the bright morning light.

When Megan saw her sister and Harrison coming into The Rise and Shine, a part of her wanted them to leave. Immediately. She knew it was out of pride; she didn't want them to see how utterly she'd failed. Especially Sara, as the business had been Megan's attempt to show Sara that she could take care of herself.

Now look at her. She'd been robbed, her bakery was a mess, and she didn't know what to say or how to feel. She felt curiously numb about it all. Shouldn't she be crying? Raging? Something?

She stood stiff as a board when Sara hugged her, and she hugged her back only because she knew Sara would expect it. Harrison placed a hand on her shoulder in solidarity, but he looked so much like Caleb that Megan had to look away.

Caleb. Of course he'd be the police officer called to the scene. Just her luck. Although she wanted to hate that Caleb was there, she also had been relieved to see him this morning. His presence had been surprisingly calm, which she attributed to his training as a police officer more than her reaction to him as a person. This was what she told herself, although a voice whispered in her mind that it had everything to with him as a person—and as a man.

"Megan, what do you want us to do?" Sara asked her. "Do you want us to help clean? Or should we call somebody? I'm not sure we can do all this on our own, especially with the glass everywhere."

Megan blinked. Cleaning. Glass. "I need to call my insurance company."

"I'll go with you to your office. Harrison, do you know somebody who can help?"

He smiled. "Why is it I'm always the one calling people?"

"Because you know everybody and their dog in this town, and you've probably gotten beers with them, too." Sara kissed his cheek before taking Megan's elbow and leading her into the back.

Sara didn't say anything, and for that, Megan was grateful. She didn't want sympathy. She wanted…she didn't know what she wanted. To find the person who did this and punch them? Run far away and never look back?

The task of calling her insurance company gave her something to do, and for that, she was grateful. She needed something concrete, something beyond thinking and worrying. Some of the feeling that had left her body slowly came back, and by the time she hung up the phone, she felt, if not renewed, at least not as numb as she had been.

Sara rubbed Megan's arm before they left the office. "Hey, look at me," she said in a soft voice. "We'll figure this out. We'll get the bakery cleaned up, and they'll find the guy who did this."

Megan wanted to tell her sister that there was no *we*. She had to do this one her own, but one look at Sara's face and she bit her tongue. She just nodded instead.

Gonzalez interviewed Megan, and she told him everything she knew, which was actually very little. She couldn't think who would've done this. She didn't have enemies—not really. Sure, maybe her next-door neighbor didn't love her that one time she accidentally left the hose on and flooded her yard, but Megan couldn't see Nora Blakely robbing her bakery for that reason.

"A cleaning crew is coming within the hour, and Officer Gonzalez has gone back to the station," Harrison announced. "But we can get started cleaning. Megan, where do you keep your trash bags and cleaning supplies?"

She showed him, and she, Sara, Harrison, and Jubilee began the clean up. As she began to rifle through her bakery's things, the anger she'd been waiting for bloomed in her chest.

A hot flush crawled up from her chest to her cheeks, and she clenched her jaw so tightly that she knew she'd have a headache later from it.

Fuck whoever did this. I'd love to take them out back and break their kneecaps.

When she picked up a piece of glass and accidentally cut herself—a light scratch—she cursed. "Fuck whoever did this!" she yelled. "Who would be this big of an asshole?"

Her question wasn't directed to anyone in particular, but she saw Sara open her mouth to answer. But before her sister could say anything, Jubilee interjected, "Clearly it was somebody who has a very sad life. He probably sits at home watching soap operas and losing bidding wars on eBay, because he collects Smurfs figurines and has an entire room dedicated to them. And when he lost out on a rare one a week ago, he decided to go robbing."

The trio stared at Jubilee. Then Harrison started laughing, which in turn caused both Megan and Sara to laugh.

"Bless you, Jubi," Sara said as she hugged the girl. "I think we all needed that."

"And I'm not sure why you think I'm not serious," Jubilee replied solemnly.

That only set off more peals of laughter, which was how Caleb found them when he returned after interviewing people next door.

"Should I ask why you're laughing?"

Megan saw him, and she had to bite her lip to keep from laughing. She shook her head. "Don't ask."

"I probably shouldn't." The gleam in his eyes dimmed slightly when he added in a quiet voice, "Megan, can I talk to you privately?"

A shiver raced up her spine at his voice. She let him take her to the back and into her office, as the cleaning crew had just arrived and had begun working on the kitchen. Caleb shut the door and turned to face her.

"I wasn't sure if you were aware, but this is the third robbery this month here in town. Unfortunately, you were hit the hardest by far." He folded his arms, grimacing. "You're lucky nothing was really stolen."

It was on the tip of her tongue to refute the idea that she was at all lucky, but she refused to let him bait her right now. When he didn't say anything, she asked, "Is that all you needed to tell me?"

His mouth twisted. "Not exactly. Due to the rash of robberies in this area, my boss wants someone to keep an eye on this block. Specifically, he wants me to watch your store, as he thinks the perpetrator will return. Since he didn't steal anything the first time around."

"You're telling me you're going to guard my *bakery*?" She scoffed. "Is that really how the police are going to use their time?"

He frowned. "I had a feeling you wouldn't be happy about this, but this isn't some random thing. We're trying to keep this area—and you—safe. Keeping watch here will make the perpetrator wary. He won't do something this brash again if he knows the police are onto his movements."

"I get that." She rubbed her arms. She knew why she was agitated: this meant that Caleb would be around. A lot. Even more than usual. Would he be outside her very door for days? Weeks? Her heart raced, and she didn't know if it was from fear or excitement.

Maybe a little of both.

"You know what? Do whatever you think you need to do," she said, exhaustion lacing her words. "I'm not going to like having you skulking around, but if it helps catch this guy, fine." She pushed past him, her shoulder bumping into his. "Just don't think I'm going to bring you coffee and a donut every morning as you sit outside my door, okay?"

He grinned that grin, the one that made her stomach flip. "Why would I expect Megan Flannigan to be nice to me? I'm not totally insane."

They stared at each other, their bodies brushing. Megan refused to acknowledge she was trembling, or that she could see golden flecks in Caleb's eyes. Or that he smelled like cedar and vetiver, and she wanted to inhale those scents until she was dizzy from them.

"Don't get in my way." She was annoyed to hear how breathy her voice was.

"And don't get in my way." He leaned down, his hot breath fanning her cheek. "Unless you want to," he said in a low voice.

She inhaled. Their gazes collided. And then before she could make another huge mistake, Megan darted from the room.

CHAPTER THREE

After they'd cleaned up the bakery as much as possible, Harrison slapped a hand on Caleb's shoulder and said he was going to take him for a drink. "You look like you need it," he said.

Caleb wasn't sure he was the person who needed a drink the most—Megan probably was the number one candidate—but he wasn't going to turn down free booze. His shift now over until morning, he let his older brother buy the first round of drinks at the Fainting Goat, a watering hole opened a few years ago in Fair Haven's small downtown.

Owned by Trent Younger, a family friend of the Thorntons, the Fainting Goat had been successful the moment it had opened its doors. Trent now owned a number of restaurants in the area, and last Caleb had heard, he was looking to open a location in Seattle. Trent also had a history with Lizzie Thornton, about which Caleb had always wondered but had never tried to pry. His younger sister, a musician traveling the country at the moment, tended to be tight-lipped about her personal life. As far as Caleb knew, she only ever confided in her twin, Seth, but with Seth overseas in the Marines…

"Hey, you two," Heath DiMarco said as he approached their table. Heath had become good friends with Harrison and Caleb ever since he'd moved to Fair Haven five years ago. A teacher who worked at Sara's elementary school, he seemed quiet and even slightly nerdy, in Caleb's opinion, with his glasses and messy hair and suits that didn't seem to fit quite right. But underneath that exterior was a man who had his own host of secrets. Caleb had yet to get Heath to tell him anything about his life before he'd moved to Fair Haven.

Caleb stared at his beer, smiling wryly. *We all have secrets, don't we?*

He most of all. Secrets that goaded him, kept him awake, and haunted his every step, no matter how many years had passed.

He tipped back his beer, letting the bitter liquid cool his throat. He didn't want to think about Megan, or her bakery, or how she'd seemed so lost until they'd started the cleanup. How he'd wanted to embrace her and let her draw on his strength for once. Watching her standing alone, her head held high and her determination clear, had cleaved him in two. Perhaps he'd wanted to let her lean on him because he had nothing else he felt he could offer her. If she rejected that, what could Megan Flannigan be to him? What could *he* be to Megan?

Caleb realized that Harrison had asked him something. "What?"

"You okay there?" His older brother peered at him. "Something happen while you were interviewing people next door?"

"Nothing happened. I can't talk specifics, but I can say that nobody saw anything." Caleb shrugged. "We're at a dead end at this point."

Heath frowned. "I'm sorry for Megan. I know how hard she's worked at that bakery. Does she need any more help cleaning up?"

Caleb bristled, and Harrison, sensing his brother was on edge, replied, "I think they've got it covered, but I'll be sure to let her know you've offered."

Staring at his drink, Caleb felt rather morose. Morose, because he felt powerless, and because the thought of Heath getting close to Megan sent him into a lather like a wild dog. Why couldn't he get her out of his mind?

"Gonzalez is fairly certain the robberies are connected," Caleb said. "It would make sense. This is a small town. Robberies like this aren't exactly commonplace to begin with, and whoever it is definitely wanted to make someone know they were pissed off at them."

"But who would do that to Megan Flannigan?" Harrison asked. "She's prickly, sure, but she's a good person. Works hard and has worked to overcome her past." He frowned at his own drink. Harrison was all too well aware of the struggles both Flannigan sisters had experienced growing up. While Sara had taken on a motherly role, Megan had rebelled until she'd gotten arrested at age seventeen for public intoxication and underage drinking. And because the universe had a wicked sense of humor, Caleb had been the one to arrest her.

"She's not exactly the nicest person." Caleb looked at both his brother and Heath, who had their eyebrows raised in question. "What? She's not. Every time we see each other, we fight."

"So are you saying you're the one who trashed her bakery?" Heath bit back a smile. "Considering she only ever fights with *you*. She's always been perfectly pleasant with me. And Harrison here. And pretty much any human and animal that comes into her bakery."

"She and I…have our issues." Caleb finished his beer and waved at the waitress. "We're working on it. And by working on it, I mean that we argue and bait each other and then go home and think about how much we hate each other."

After they gave their orders for a second round, Harrison said, "You know, I've always thought that hate and love were related."

Caleb groaned. "Not this again."

"No, I want to hear this," Heath said. "What's your theory?"

"Only that love and hate both make people do stupid things, and they both bring out strong emotions. If you love somebody, you care about them; if you hate somebody, you care about them, in a twisted kind of way. You have a connection." Harrison sipped his beer in thoughtful silence.

"So you're saying, what? That Megan and I actually love each other?"

"No, not necessarily. Just that you two clearly have some kind of connection, no matter how much you try to deny it," Harrison said. "It's been ten years since you arrested her. You'd think by now any anger would've settled and passed."

"It is strange that she would hold that against you," Heath said. "It's not like you committed a crime. She screwed up, you did your job. End of story. And she was lucky that the charges were dropped, right?"

Caleb didn't want to think about that night, when he'd just

joined the force and been called to a party that had gotten out of hand on the outskirts of town. When he'd arrived, he'd recognized multiple high school students, and there'd been drugs, booze, and God knew what else. Caleb hadn't wanted to arrest any of those kids for being young and stupid and loud, but Megan Flannigan had been drunk off of her ass. A month away from turning eighteen, she was underage and also completely wasted. She'd decided to pick a fight with him, and when she'd pushed him—barely moving him an inch, she was so off-balance—he'd known he'd have to take her in. Mostly for her own safety. He'd seen the looks some of the college guys had given her. He'd known what could happen to a vulnerable teenage girl at these types of parties.

So Caleb had arrested her, taken her to the small Fair Haven jail, and kept her until she'd sobered up. Since it was Megan, it hadn't been so simple as waiting for her to sober up.

It never was with her.

Ever since that night, she'd hated him. She'd made no secret of that fact. The irony? She had no idea that the guy she had taunted as a stick in the mud and as a boring prude had done something even more stupid, more damaging. More devastating. Something that made him feel like a fraud every day he worked as a police officer, adhering to the rules, when he'd skirted the rules that night and every night since.

"As I've learned with the Flannigan sisters," Harrison said wryly, "there's probably another side to the story. Probably twenty different sides. They're a mysterious pair."

"Not so mysterious that Sara didn't make the very terrible decision to get engaged to you." Caleb couldn't stop himself from needling his brother, who was also ridiculously in love with his fiancée. "You two have a wedding date set? And why am I asking that at all?" He looked at Heath. "You see what happens when one of us gets caught? We all start to fall in line."

"Next you'll be shopping for bridesmaids dresses," Heath rejoined with a grin. "What's your favorite color for a wedding, Caleb? I'm partial to blues, if I'm being honest."

"Shut the hell up, you two," Harrison growled, although based on the smile on his face, he wasn't really annoyed. "The day you two fall in love is the day I make a national holiday to rub your noses in the dirt."

"Ease off, old man." Caleb lifted his glass. "A toast to Harrison and Sara: may we all be lucky enough to find a woman to put up with us."

"I'll drink to that," Heath said.

The trio clinked glasses before Harrison began to talk about Sara, her young son James, wedding planning, Harrison and Caleb's mother Lisa's antipathy toward Sara that was only now starting to defrost, and a discussion of the merits of a spring wedding versus a summer wedding. Caleb's mind drifted, mostly to the one topic that he could never seem to get away from. It didn't help that Harrison was marrying Megan's sister: that just meant he was tied to the Flannigan sisters even if he didn't want to be. Caleb couldn't stop himself from imagining Megan getting married. Would she wear a traditional wedding dress? He had a feeling she'd wear something different. Something colorful.

He blanched when an image of Megan in a wedding gown popped into his mind. He almost groaned out loud. What the hell was wrong with him? He needed an exorcism. Or at least another beer.

An hour later, Heath said his goodbyes, leaving Harrison

and Caleb alone. The two brothers sat in companionable silence. As the first and second eldest of the Thornton siblings, they'd had their share of responsibilities growing up in a family as lively and dynamic as theirs. With four younger siblings, they'd taken on the protective brother roles from the very beginning, especially when Jubilee had been going through cancer treatments as a young girl.

Mark, the third oldest, had preferred his own company and had left Fair Haven for his own kind of haven on a ranch down south; Lizzie, the fourth eldest, had been too pretty and talented for her own good, but she'd run off to pursue her musical dreams right after high school and after she'd broken up with Trent Younger; Seth, the fifth eldest and Lizzie's twin, had been inseparable from his twin until they'd parted ways after high school when he'd joined the Marines; and then Jubilee, the sixth and youngest, was the baby of the family who'd been coddled due to her childhood leukemia that had returned when she was thirteen.

"So you're going to be a security guard now?" Harrison asked with a raised brow. "And at Megan's bakery?"

"Hilarious, right?"

"Was it really your boss's idea for you to be given that position, or did you have some hand in it?"

Caleb stilled. "What are you saying?"

"Exactly what I just said. Everyone has seen how you react when you're around Megan. You don't see anyone else in the room." Harrison finished off his beer and pushed it away across the table. "A word of advice?"

"Do I have a choice?"

"Nope, so listen up. This bickering with her? The arguments and fighting and whatever it is you two have decided is some kind of foreplay? Either get to the deed, or let it go. Either ask her out once and for all, or leave her alone."

Caleb gritted his teeth. "It's not like that."

"Really? You could've fooled me." Harrison lowered his voice. "Look, you're my brother, and my best friend, besides Sara. I know how you tick, and I think you'd say the same about me. Don't let what happened years ago keep you from getting what you want. Don't ignore feelings you have for Megan out of some kind of misplaced guilt."

Caleb's throat went dry, and his heart started pounding. He pushed the memories away—the crash, the sirens, the screaming—and he had to close his eyes for a moment. "I don't have feelings for her," was all he could say.

"I won't argue with you, but, just think about what I said. Okay?" Harrison bumped shoulders with him. "I want to see you happy."

"Since when did you turn into Oprah?"

"Since I found the best woman to love." Harrison's lips quirked into a grin. "Now, are you going to buy the next round or not?"

MEGAN HADN'T WANTED to go to dinner with her family and Harrison tonight, but Sara had convinced her to come along. They'd decided to eat at Harrison's place, mostly because it was easily three times the size of Sara's house, which she shared with their mother Ruth and Sara's son James. Everyone chatted as they ate, but Megan found herself pushing her food around on her plate.

She couldn't stop thinking about her bakery. She felt like

she'd left her child behind when she'd closed up last night, after they'd cleaned up as much as they could before dropping from exhaustion. She'd returned that morning to finish the cleanup and work with Jubilee to order ingredients that had been dumped or damaged.

It hadn't helped that Caleb had been lurking the entire time she'd been at the bakery today. When he'd told her he was going to watch over the bakery, he'd really meant it. Megan was torn between frustration and gratitude for his help. She couldn't help but feel safe with him right outside. She might not like the guy, but she'd never doubt his efficacy as a police officer and his ability to protect people.

She pushed her green beans to the corner of her plate. Looking up, she saw Sara's concerned gaze on her. Seated right next to each other, the sisters had only hugged before helping Harrison get dinner ready.

"You doing okay?" Sara asked in a low voice. "You look like you could fall asleep right here."

Megan laughed, but it was a sad sound. "I can't stop thinking about everything I have to get done. I couldn't sleep last night, and I ended up getting up at three AM to make a list of things to do." She barely stifled a wide yawn.

"You're already making amazing progress. You'll reopen next week, right?" Sara rubbed Megan's arm. "You got this."

Megan smiled. Her older sister had always been her number one supporter, and she knew only too well how lucky she'd been to have a sister who'd looked out for her while their mother couldn't.

Their mother Ruth had given them their blue eyes and freckled skin, but—at least in Megan's eyes—little beyond that. Ruth had been an alcoholic throughout the majority of

Sara and Megan's childhood, only getting sober within the last few years. Sara had mostly forgiven Ruth for what she'd put them through, but Megan hadn't gotten to that place yet. She was civil to her mother, but she had no real desire to have a relationship with her. How could Ruth make up for the days and nights where she'd been so drunk that she'd collapsed onto the couch and not wake up for what felt like days? The stints in rehab that never stuck? The humiliation of having a parent come drunk to a parent-teacher conference? Or when a friend's parents had to drive the girls home from school because Ruth was passed out drunk at a bar somewhere, and they'd missed the bus?

Megan had never been very good with forgiveness. She knew all too well it was one of her worst faults. She often felt that forgiveness was akin to *forgetting*, and she could never forget. It wasn't in her DNA.

"You've barely eaten anything," Ruth said, pointing at Megan's plate. "Makes me think of how you'd try to hide your vegetables in your sleeve when you were little."

Megan swallowed the retort that sat on her tongue, wanting to remind her mother that there had been few dinners where she would've even noticed Megan's vegetable-hiding underneath the haze of booze.

"I'm just tired. Sorry I'm such terrible company," she said instead.

"Are you sad about your store?" James asked. James, at the age of six, had just finished first grade and was growing like a weed. Nobody knew where he was getting his burst of height from—Sara was average height and so was James's father. James liked to say that he got his height from his soon-to-be stepfather Harrison.

"Yeah, I am sad," Megan replied. "I can't stop thinking about it."

James nodded sagely. "I told Travis what happened. You know my friend Travis? He says that it was probably ninjas. He saw something on TV about how ninjas can hide in the shadows and you wouldn't even know it."

Everyone laughed, including Megan.

"Where does Travis come up with these things?" Harrison ruffled James's hair. "Sometimes I think you shouldn't hang out with him. He says the craziest things."

"No, Travis is my friend! Mom, you won't let Harrison do that, right? And you messed up my hair."

Sara replied seriously, "No, of course not. Besides, he lives right next door, so I don't think I could keep him away anyway."

James returned to eating, but not before he fixed his hair. He'd decided a week ago that he wanted his hair spiked with hair gel, and after persuading his mom that it was *very important*, he had perfectly coifed hair everywhere he went. He also hated when anyone messed it up.

Megan felt her mood lighten a little. Her family was exhausting, but they were good people. She was happy to see Sara so happy, too: after her divorce, she'd been too afraid to let herself love Harrison, but he'd shown her it was worth it. He adored Sara, and Megan was both glad and a little bit jealous of their relationship.

What would it be like to have a man love you that much? She couldn't imagine it.

Unbidden, an image of Caleb's face came into her mind, but she brushed it away. *He's never going to be that man for you. No matter how much you may want it.*

Yes, she wanted Caleb. She'd admitted that to herself long ago, although outwardly, she acted like she hated him. It was easier than acknowledging that he'd hurt her—multiple times. It was easier than accepting that he'd never care for her in that way. He'd rejected her—and arrested her!—enough times for her to get the hint.

Now her mood shifted back to morose. When dessert was brought out, Megan declined a piece of cake.

"You sure, honey?" Ruth prodded. "Here, come on, have a little piece. Your sister went to a lot of trouble to make it, and you need to eat something." She pushed the plate before Megan and patted her shoulder before sitting down.

It was strange to have Ruth act like a mother. How could she act like nothing had happened before? Megan gritted her teeth, the old hurt welling up inside her chest.

"Isn't carrot cake your favorite?" Ruth asked. "I thought you loved carrot cake."

Megan couldn't stop the memory from welling inside her: for her eighth birthday, she'd asked Ruth to make her a carrot cake. She'd loved carrot cake. Ruth had agreed, and she'd promised that she make it for Megan's birthday, along with having a party with friends.

Ruth had dreamed up the greatest party—a piñata, pin the tail on the donkey, gifts galore—and Megan had barely been able to sleep, she'd been so excited for the following morning. Yet when she'd woken up, she hadn't seen any kind of party preparations. Megan found Ruth sprawled on her bed, an empty bottle of vodka next to her, and Megan had known that there would be no party. No gifts, no friends, no piñata. No carrot cake.

It was stupid, to feel hurt over something like that. Megan

hated that Ruth could hurt her, even now. She was twenty-seven. How could she continue to cry over the fact that she didn't have a birthday party over twenty years ago?

"Actually, I hate carrot cake." Megan pushed her cake aside and rose. "I've hated it ever since you promised to make me one on my eighth birthday but were too drunk the next morning to even get out of bed."

Ruth paled, her hand going to her throat. She swallowed. "Megan…" she murmured.

Megan looked at Sara, who looked unbearably sad. "Thank you for dinner. I need to get going."

She kissed James goodbye before she headed out.

As she drove home, she knew she shouldn't have said that to Ruth. It had been a low shot, and unfair. Ruth had only been concerned about her wellbeing. Yet the little girl inside Megan rejoiced that she'd said it. Perhaps it was immature, but she refused to feel guilty about it. At least not yet. In the morning, when Sara would call her and ask why she'd said that, she'd say she was sorry.

Megan winced. *I really fucked up, didn't I?*

She was always going to be the screw-up, wasn't she? Arrested at seventeen, her bakery almost destroyed, and lashing out at her mother at a family dinner. The feelings of inadequacy pushed at her, almost choking her. After her arrest, she'd lost her scholarship to the University of Washington, and she'd hated Caleb for it for years. It hadn't been fair to him, of course. But his arresting her had revealed a side of her she'd feared becoming for years: just like Ruth. Drunk, disorderly, and a failure. He'd made her confront that side of herself—and she'd blamed him for it.

When would she ever feel like she wasn't a failure?

After getting home, she collapsed onto the couch. Her cat Gary jumped onto her lap, purring like a motor cage. Gary was orange and white striped with a smashed face and a propensity to drool when you scratched his cheeks. He was Megan's best friend. Or at least the creature with whom she spent the most time lately.

"Did I fuck up, Gare-bear?" she asked the cat. "Should I call and apologize?"

Gary kneaded her legs. She scratched behind his ears just to hear him purr louder.

She'd call in the morning. She'd apologize to everyone, and she'd try to make things right with Ruth. Sara had wanted Megan to work on her issues with their mother for years, but Megan had always resisted it. What did it matter? The past was the past.

And yet, despite everything, the past always managed to bleed into the present no matter how much you tried to staunch the old wounds.

For the strangest reason, Megan wanted to talk to Caleb. To feel his protective presence, to allow herself to lean on him. Physically, emotionally. Her emotions regarding Caleb Thornton were as tangled as a skein of knotted yarn, and sometimes she didn't know if she resented him or wanted him more.

Gary finally curled into a ball on her lap. Megan stroked his soft fur as the night pushed onward, not sure of anything anymore.

CHAPTER FOUR

"**I**s he seriously going to stand out there all day?" Megan asked in irritation as she wiped down the counter.

Jubilee glanced at her before smiling at the customer in front of her. Once she gave the older woman her cinnamon roll and coffee, she replied, "He's doing his job, you know."

Megan made a face. If doing his job meant being a giant pain in the ass, then Caleb was doing a great job.

She watched as he leaned against a light post, his hands in his pockets. He looked deceptively nonchalant, but she knew he was capable of moving at lightning speed if necessary. When she'd come to the bakery that morning, he'd already been outside, sitting in his car and watching over the bakery and the neighborhood overall. She didn't really understand how this was going to help them uncover the perpetrator, but then again, if it kept her bakery safe from another robbery, she wouldn't complain. At least not too much.

"I heard about what happened," the next customer said, a young woman with bouncy blonde curls who Megan didn't recognize. "Was a ton of stuff stolen? Did you see who did it? Are you scared to be here now?"

Megan opened her mouth to say that if she'd seen who'd done this Caleb wouldn't have to stand watch, but Jubilee replied first. "We didn't see who it was, no. It happened during the night."

The girl pouted. "That's boring." Her eyes widened as she looked out the window, which had since been repaired at no cost by one of Harrison's many friends. "But how lucky you are to have Officer Thornton close by! He's so yummy. I love a man in uniform."

Jubilee smiled while Megan returned to wiping down her counter. Aggressively.

"Well, he's my brother, so I don't have an opinion about that," Jubilee said brightly, "but we do appreciate how helpful the police have been. Haven't we, Megan?"

"Oh, yes, they've been great. Almost too great."

She saw Caleb out of the corner of her eye, and it only made her bristle. She was like a hedgehog around him, all prickles and thorns, and part of her found it rather exhausting. But then she remembered what had happened between them, and she couldn't find it in her heart to give up her antipathy toward him. Maybe in another life things could've been different. *Or maybe pigs really do fly*, Megan thought wryly.

The blonde girl bounced out of the bakery with her coffee. Customers steadily came in, allowing Megan to stop thinking about the police officer lurking outside. As the day wore on, she couldn't help but wonder why he felt the need to stand outside when he could sit in his car, and if he were sweating like crazy under the hot sun. It was unnaturally warm today, especially for Fair Haven, which had fairly mild summers. The temperature edged toward ninety degrees by mid-afternoon, and Caleb didn't move from his post.

"Do you think he's hot?" Megan ventured before she could rethink her question.

Jubilee raised an eyebrow. She looked so much like Caleb in that gesture that Megan's heart twisted. "Probably. It's hot out today. Although Caleb likes to act like he's some kind of superhero, though. He'd never admit he was uncomfortable."

Megan watched as Caleb wiped his forehead. The sun beat down, and, suddenly irritated with both herself and him, she grabbed a cup of cold lemonade and a sandwich from the case and went outside.

"Here," she said, handing him the lemonade and sandwich. "You look like you need it."

He stared at the proffered items. "Should I be worried?"

"What, that I poisoned them? Don't be a jerk." She slapped the sandwich against his chest and was rather tempted to dump the lemonade on his boots, but he took the cup from her hand with a smile.

"Thank you." He sipped the lemonade, and she couldn't stop herself from staring at how he swallowed. How his Adam's apple bobbed, and how he had dark stubble on his jaw and throat.

Her mouth went dry.

"Well, I should get back inside." She felt awkward now, like she didn't know where to put her arms. At her sides? Crossed in front of her? She felt ungainly, like a newborn colt, and she hated feeling out of sorts. Caleb never failed to make her feel just like that—unsure and unbalanced.

"Don't go yet." He sat down on a bench in front of her bakery. "Jubilee's in there, right? Have you taken a break yet today?"

She realized she hadn't, and her stomach rumbled in reminder that she hadn't eaten. He smiled when he heard the sound. Her cheeks heated.

"We were busy today. Which is good. I'm glad that the robbery hasn't kept people away," she babbled.

He held out half of the sandwich, which she took after a moment's hesitation. Biting into the roast beef and watercress sandwich, she almost moaned in relief. She'd been hungrier than she'd realized. He ate his half, and they sat in companionable silence, gazing out onto the quiet main street that held most of Fair Haven's restaurants and shops. A tiny town north of Seattle on the Puget Sound, Fair Haven was famous for its lakes and its charm. Although Megan often found Fair Haven rather too quiet—and she'd wanted to leave its environs when she'd been younger—she found herself enjoying its peacefulness today.

Even if that meant living in the same town as Caleb Thornton.

"Have you guys discovered anything new?" she asked as she finished off the sandwich. "Any new leads?"

He shook his head. "Nothing yet." He looked at her and added wryly, "I know you don't love me hanging around, but it's for your protection, you know. We don't know what this guy will do next, except that based on the robbery, there's a decent likelihood he'll come back."

Her heart clenched at his words. *For your protection.* She could count on one hand when she'd felt like she could rely on someone for safety growing up. Ruth had been too drunk, and although Sara had done her best, she'd only been a kid, too.

They gazed at each other, the sun almost painfully bright, and Megan couldn't stop the wish that if she could change the past, she would. If only to have Caleb never stop looking at her the way he was looking at her right now.

"I know I haven't always been the nicest," she admitted, which caused Caleb to snort. She glared at him. "But you—and the entire force—have been great. Really. I appreciate it." The words tripped from her tongue, like they didn't want to be admitted, but she needed to say it. She didn't want him to think she was some ungrateful brat, even if most of the time she wanted to kick him in the shins.

"'Not the nicest?'" He grinned. "How about completely terrifying?"

She narrowed her eyes. "Don't push your luck."

"Any other guy would be trembling in his boots, you know. You could scare Captain America himself with that scowl. Yes, that one, exactly."

She moved to push him, but he laughed and moved out of the way, which caused her to pitch forward. He caught her, his strong fingers around her wrists, and she gazed up into his green eyes, unable to look away. His hands were warm and callused, and he smelled like sweat and male. She wanted to push the dark hair from his forehead.

"Megan…"

That voice—how he said her name. Memories came to her, and she couldn't push them away no matter how much she wanted to. This wasn't the first time that they'd been this close. Not even the second time. Oh, she and Caleb had a history, all right, and she hated that that history could never be erased.

The night Caleb had arrested her, Megan had been drunk. Angry. And she'd had a crush the size of Texas on the handsome Caleb Thornton, who was twenty-three to her seventeen. After he'd booked her and they'd waited for somebody to come get her out of jail—unlikely, given that Ruth was too flakey and Sara lived in Seattle then—Megan had wanted to push him. Test him. Test herself. Maybe it had been the alcohol, or her arrest, or sheer stupidity. But when he'd entered her cell that night, she'd wrapped herself around him and kissed him. He'd been so warm and solid that she'd wanted to melt into him.

He'd frozen in her arms, and then when she'd tried to deepen the kiss, he'd set her away from him. And then he'd said the words she'd never forget: *Get ahold of yourself. You're acting like a spoiled child.* He'd looked disgusted before he'd stalked out of her cell, leaving her to feel the full ache of her humiliation and, yes, guilt.

Years later, she'd known she'd been a complete idiot, and that his reaction had been her fault completely. Not only had she been drunk in public, but she'd thrown herself at an officer. Deep down inside, she'd still harbored a crush for Caleb Thornton, and it had only grown in size as she'd gotten older. Even after one boyfriend and a second had come and gone, he'd been there, forever in her heart.

Now, though, he didn't look at her with disgust. He looked at her like a man wanted a woman. The realization thrilled her.

He'd looked at her like that a year ago. A year ago when they'd kissed outside the Fainting Goat. That kiss had been burned into her memory, and she'd dreamt of it so many times she'd lost count. The way his lips had brushed over hers, how he'd touched his tongue to hers. How she'd shivered, yet the night had been almost balmy. Yet that time, Megan had pushed him away, telling him she couldn't do this. *This isn't good*, she'd said lamely. She hadn't even known what she'd meant. Caleb, his eyes dark, hadn't protested. He'd stepped aside and let her go, even though deep inside, she'd wanted him to take her home.

A car honked in the distance, jolting them apart in the present moment. The lemonade sloshed onto Caleb's hand, and Megan scrambled off the bench. She couldn't do this. What was she thinking? That things could be different?

She almost laughed. When would she ever learn?

Caleb wiped his hand on his uniform. Megan turned to go, but his voice stopped her.

"Wait." He touched her arm.

She waited, not looking at him. "What?"

"I just…I don't know." He sounded frustrated. "I know things haven't been great between us for a long time, but maybe—"

"Maybe we could forget everything that's happened?" She shrugged, her heart cracking a little. "I doubt it."

"God, you drive me crazy." His voice was a growl. "I can't ever tell what you want. One moment you kiss me, the next you hate me."

She whirled. "And who's fault is that? You've never acted like you wanted me. You've always acted like you couldn't stand me."

"I don't—I mean, no." He raked his hands through his hair. "If you'd give a guy half a chance, Megan."

She shook her head. "I have to go back inside. Enjoy your lemonade."

She didn't stop to hear what he had to say next. Rushing inside, she refused to look at Jubilee, who she was sure had seen—and heard—everything that had happened. She groaned inwardly. When would she stop making a cake out of herself over Caleb Thornton?

She was grateful when the after-school rush kept them both busy. By the time they had a break, it was time to close up for the evening. And by then, Caleb had been replaced by another police officer who sat in his car instead of standing outside.

"You know, as someone who's related to Caleb," Jubilee began in a nonchalant tone, "you should know that he isn't the type of guy to show interest in a woman if he isn't, you know, interested."

Megan narrowed her eyes. She tossed stale bagels into the trash with extra gusto. "Your brother is a menace."

"That's true, although he's not the worst of the four." Jubilee tapped her chin. "I may not be an expert on human behavior, but I'd say there's a reason why he won't stop bothering you."

"He has a brain disease?"

Jubilee laughed. "Sure, that's one way to call it." She batted her eyelashes at Megan. "If you call *liking somebody* a brain disease."

Megan groaned. "Not this again, Jubilee. He doesn't like me. Or want me. Or want to date me." A flush crawled up her face, and she was annoyed by it. He might want her for sex, but he'd never shown her that he wanted her for anything else. Besides, he'd rejected her once already. She'd rejected him, too, and God above, it was a total mess, wasn't it?

A small voice whispered that she refused to consider him because if she were wrong—if *he* rejected *her* a second time— she didn't know if she could survive the heartbreak. She wanted him so much that she'd rather never know that he'd never wanted her. It was stupid and twisted, and she wished she could unknot her feelings without leaving bruises behind.

"It would never work anyway," she said, more to herself than Jubilee. "We fight all the time. We'd be arguing every chance we got." Jubilee opened her mouth to argue, but Megan held up a hand. "Seriously. I don't want to talk about it anymore, okay? I know you and everybody else think that we're destined to be together or something, but there are things you don't know."Jubilee's eyes widened. "Like what? Secrets? You can't tease me like that!"

Megan couldn't help from laughing. She shook her head, pointing at the kitchen. "Go clean up so we can get out of here before midnight."

"Fine, but don't think I'm going to forget about this!"

Megan wished she could forget about everything. Then again, would she really want to forget? Although she was ashamed of what had happened ten years ago, with her arrest and her throwing herself at Caleb, she also knew that that had been the night when she'd really grown up. Before then, she'd relied on Sara, who'd been the adult for most of Megan's life. Megan had coasted through life, angry at Ruth and so sure that Sara would clean up her mess. But after her arrest and the loss of her scholarship, Megan had had to come to terms with the fact that her actions had consequences. She'd wanted to blame Caleb—and for a while, she had—but she'd eventually been forced to accept that she'd had no one but herself to blame. She'd gotten her life together and started her bakery, refusing to let herself be defeated by her own mistakes.

As she closed up The Rise and Shine and said goodbye to Jubilee, Megan wondered if she'd be where she was today without Caleb Thornton. Despite her best efforts, her life would be forever intertwined with his, no matter how hard she twisted and turned to free herself of him.

CHAPTER FIVE

Caleb leaned his head against The Rise and Shine's brick wall and restrained himself from banging his head against said wall. It would certainly be less painful than whatever it was he was doing with Megan Flannigan.

It'd been two weeks since the robbery, and although there had yet to be any real leads as to the perpetrator, Caleb was still tasked with watching the bakery and the surrounding businesses. They had gotten more than one tip of another possible robbery in the vicinity, and as a result, Caleb's presence was supposed to deter any more crime occurring.

So he told himself. He rather felt like he was like some guardian angel, except the woman he was watching wanted nothing to do with him.

He let out a breath. It was his own fault, really. He and Megan had always been at odds—even when they'd been kissing.

Now he really wanted to bang his head against the wall.

He'd rejected Megan when she'd tried to kiss him after he'd arrested her. He had to: she was underage—albeit a month shy of turning eighteen—and he'd been twenty-three and just newly added to the police force. He couldn't screw everything up by reciprocating her interest, despite the fact that she was beautiful, with that red hair and blue eyes and even her sharp tongue. He'd pushed her aside, told her she was being childish, and stuffed every feeling he'd ever thought about Megan so far down inside he'd almost convinced himself those feelings had never existed.

When she'd ended up hating him, part of him had been glad. If she hated him, then he wouldn't pursue her. She wasn't the type of woman he should pursue—she wasn't interested in playing by the rules, and he needed a woman who did just that.

He had to play by the rules because when he hadn't, it had resulted in tragedy.

He closed his eyes. He didn't want to remember, but he had to. This was his atonement, his sin, his secret. When he'd been all of sixteen—almost the same age as when Megan had been arrested—he killed his best friend. He and Daniel had both been drunk and been at a raucous party until the wee hours of the morning. Caleb had never been a big drinker, but he'd wanted to fit in that night. Besides, Daniel had been drinking, and the two of them were two peas in a pod, as their mothers liked to call them. Caleb had been slightly less drunk than Daniel, and he'd offered to drive Daniel and himself home.

Daniel never made it home.

On the twisting road home, a deer had shot out into the road. Caleb had slammed on the brakes, but the road had been wet and the car's tires had been worn down. He'd fishtailed straight into a tree. Daniel had been killed instantly by the impact. Caleb, though? He'd survived with only a broken finger and a mild concussion.

The worst part was that Caleb had been conscious the entire time. Stuck in that mangled car, screaming Daniel's name. The ambulance had arrived, and they'd pulled Caleb and Daniel free of the wreckage. Caleb hadn't known that his friend had been dead the entire time he'd been stuck in that car until the following morning, when his parents had come into his hospital room and had told him with low voices and gray faces.

Because he was a Thornton—rich, privileged, and very much concerned with image—his parents had hidden Caleb's crime from the public. As a juvenile, his records had been sealed, and he'd gotten off with nothing worse than probation, community service, and a hefty fine, mostly due to his parents' influence in the community. Added to the fact that no one had seen the two boys leave the party together, and Caleb's injuries had been minor enough to be explained from another source.

Caleb had wanted to tell people. He'd wanted to confess, to tell the world that he'd killed his best friend. He had blood on his hands. The guilt consumed him until he didn't know how he'd survive with it on his shoulders.

But Lisa Thornton, the indomitable matriarch of the Thornton family, had persuaded Caleb to keep everything quiet. *Why ruin your future over this?* she'd reasoned. *You could lose your scholarship to UCLA. Would Daniel have wanted that for you?*

Heartbroken, lost and angry, he'd agreed. He hadn't attended Daniel's funeral. He regretted that the most. And as the years passed, he'd become all too aware of how he was a fraud. How he put on his uniform every morning, acting like he hadn't killed his friend while driving drunk. How he'd survived and Daniel hadn't.

He should've been the one to die. He'd been the driver. If there'd been any justice, the universe would have taken him instead of Daniel.

The only people who knew of Caleb's secret were his parents and Harrison. To everyone else, Daniel had died in his own car after careening off of a wet road into a tree. The only small mercy had been the fact that nothing about Daniel drinking had been released to the media. The town mourned Daniel Finley's death as a tragic accident, and then he was forgotten, except for the occasional sad shake of the head if he were mentioned. *So young. His poor mother.*

After college, Caleb had returned to Fair Haven and had decided to become a police officer. He'd live the rest of his life doing the right thing, he'd reasoned. Yet no matter how much time had passed, it hadn't alleviated the gaping, bitter wound of him causing Daniel's death.

That was why he needed to leave Megan alone. He could tell himself it was because she wasn't the right type of woman for him, but in reality, he knew she'd hate him when she found out what he'd done. She'd grown up with an alcoholic mother. Would she want to be with a guy who'd killed his friend while drinking and driving? And who'd arrested her for the same crime years later?

Yet only a year ago, he'd kissed her. He'd kissed her like he'd always wanted to kiss her, and in the deepest parts of his soul, he couldn't make himself regret it.

Last summer, Megan had been at a table with her sister Sara and a few other women at the Fainting Goat, laughing and drinking. Her hair had been loose around her shoulders like a river of fire, and when he had sat down at a corner booth, he hadn't been able to stop himself from watching her.

Watching the way she tipped her head back as she laughed; how melodious her voice was. How she moved with a fluidity that captivated him, how she seemed to energize every space she occupied. How her slim fingers clasped her drink, and how her shirt rode up slightly each time she moved, exposing her pale lower back.

He drank and he watched her, wishing he were anyone else. Wishing he didn't care so much. Wishing he could drink until he pushed every memory aside like a bad dream.

He watched as she went outside to take a call because she couldn't get service inside the bar. He hadn't meant to follow her. He told himself to leave her alone, but it was like a tether linked them together no matter how hard he fought against it.

When he went outside, he found her with a man he didn't recognize. Jealousy sparked in his gut. The jealousy turned to rage when he realized the man had decided to accost her for simply being female in a public place.

"Look, I'm not going to give you my number," she said. She was firm and calm, but he saw in her body language how uncomfortable she was. "Leave me alone."

"You dress like that and you won't give me your number?" the man sneered. "Why are all of you women such teases? I don't get it. What's a guy gotta do to get you bitches to be nice for once?"

Caleb didn't waste time. He took the man by the collar, slamming him against the wall. He barely heard Megan's gasp of surprise. "Get the hell out of here before I permanently rearrange your face," he said.

The man sputtered and tried to explain, but Caleb just

tightened his grip. The man nodded, and with a wheeze, he wrenched free and darted off into the night.

"You really didn't need to do that," Megan said behind him, her tone clearly annoyed. "I can take care of myself."

"Obviously you can't, if you can't rid of guys like that."

She visibly bristled, and he couldn't help but think she was beautiful when she was angry: flushed, her eyes narrowed, and, yes, her breasts pushed up against her shirt. *God, I'm an animal, aren't I?*

"Okay, well, thanks for your assistance, Officer. You can go now."

He moved so only a fingers-width of space separated them. Her eyes widened in surprise, but satisfaction rose inside him when she didn't tell him to back away. If anything, her breathing only increased, and he saw her nipples tighten through her shirt.

"I don't want to go. How about I stay out here with you?" He pressed a hand above her head against the wall.

"Why would you want to do that?"

"Do you really have to ask that question?"

Her eyes narrowed, which only made him want to smile, as it was the classic annoyed-Megan-Flannigan look. "So now you're talking in riddles? Are you Dr. Seuss? Go away and bug someone else with your Green-Eggs-and-Ham act, Caleb."

He smiled. "'Would you eat them/In a box?/Would you eat them/With a fox?'" he recited.

Despite herself, a smile curved her red lips. "Do I want to know why you know that by heart?"

"'So I will eat them in a box./And I will eat them with a fox./And I will eat them in a house,'" he continued, pressing closer until only a breath separated them now. His heart pounded in his ears, and her sweet scent filled his nose. His body hardened despite himself.

"'And I will eat them with a mouse./And I will eat them here and there./Say! I will eat them anywhere!'" He finished with a murmur next to her ear, "'I do so like/Green eggs and ham!/Thank you!/Thank you, Sam-I-am.'" Brushing a thumb across her lower lip, he thrilled when she trembled ever so slightly. And when the tip of her tongue touched his thumb?

All of his self-control shattered.

Cupping her face, he kissed her. Her lips were petal-soft, and she gasped when his mouth captured hers. But it was a gasp of want, of desperation, and it only fueled those feelings in him. He caressed her jaw, urging her to open for him, and when she surrendered, he felt a wellspring of emotion flood through his body.

He wrapped his arms around her. Not caring that they were in public, outside, that he'd told himself he'd leave her alone, that she could never be the woman for him—he kissed her anyway. Maybe he kissed her *because* of those things. Maybe he wanted her so much because he knew he could never have her. And yet, he knew that no matter the circumstances, she would never leave his heart.

He didn't know if this was love. It was lust, a roaring kind of desire that he'd never experienced with another woman.

Their bodies pressed together, and he felt her soft breasts against his chest. She was taller than most women, but he was almost half a head taller than her. She stood on her tiptoes to get closer to him. He loved that. He loved how she tasted, how she felt underneath his fingers. How she responded to every movement of his mouth against her own.

He couldn't get enough of her. How had he denied himself for this long?

When someone coughed, they broke apart. Megan's eyes widened, like she'd just gotten caught doing something wrong, and his gut twisted. *Of course she doesn't really want me. She's always hated me, hasn't she?* It was an obnoxiously cynical thought, but it settled inside him like a scaly snake.

"I need to go back inside. They're probably looking for me." She ducked under his arm, but she stopped before she returned inside the bar.

She looked over her shoulder at him. "This can't happen again." Before he could respond, or tell her she was wrong, she hurried inside like she'd just escaped the clutches of some villain.

When he arrived home, Caleb almost considered getting drunk, something he hadn't done since the night Daniel had died. Although he drank alcohol from time to time, he never, ever got drunk. Instead, he decided to go running at the crack of dawn until he was so tired he couldn't move.

The present rushed back into him when he heard a smoke detector start screaming. Rushing inside the bakery, he smelled smoke coming from the kitchen.

"Everyone, go outside!" he yelled to the patrons. They hurried outside as Caleb used his radio to call for backup. He searched for Megan, but he realized with rising horror that she must be in the kitchen.

"Megan! Where are you?" The kitchen was hazy with smoke, but not enough that he was completely blinded. He saw Megan grab a nearby fire extinguisher, and she sprayed the oven that was belching smoke. White stuff soon covered not only the oven but the counters and floor, too. Once the fire was out, Megan stood gasping. Caleb felt rather foolish for having overreacted over what had obviously been a small fire.

They both heard the sirens. Megan's eyes widened. "Why did you call 911?"

"Because there was a fire," he replied, surly.

Embarrassed, he left to speak to the firefighters who were about to invade the bakery. The last thing anyone needed was a bunch of water damage from spraying hoses.

The firemen inspected the damage and made certain all sparks were put out, but luckily, nothing but the oven had really been scorched.

"Looks like you had something that caught fire at the bottom of the oven?" one of the firemen told Megan. "Be careful about that. This could've been much worse than it was."

She nodded. "Stupid mistake. Sorry for making you guys come out here, but thanks for your help."

Caleb and Megan opened the windows and doors to help clear the smoke. The patrons outside were assured that despite the now smoky scent permeating the kitchen, everything was fine. To Caleb's relief, Jubilee arrived soon after, and she assured them both she could run the front in order to allow Megan time to clean up the kitchen.

Caleb didn't know why he stayed with Megan. Maybe because he'd seen the defeated slump of her shoulders, or because she'd been through so much lately. He watched as she got a broom and began to clean up the mess, but when he saw the broom was trembling in her hand, he took it from her.

"Megan," he said in a low voice. "Are you okay?"

He knew it was a stupid question, and he expected her to

rail at him. To his astonishment, he saw tears sparkle in her eyes.

"No, I'm not okay. I'm tired of this, and I'm tired of being terrified that in the next breath my business is going to be fucking *destroyed*—" She took a deep breath, but the next exhale came out as a sob.

Caleb didn't think: he reacted. Taking her into his arms, he held her close. She didn't resist, which showed him how much she needed to be comforted right now. Laying her head on his chest, she cried, her entire body shaking. He rubbed her back and said soothing nothings into her ear, wishing he could make all of this disappear.

He eventually guided her to her office and, after getting her a glass of water, told her to sit down. "Jubilee will take care of things," he said in a firm voice when she looked like she would argue.

He sat down across from her, although he took her hands and rubbed them in gentle strokes. She seemed to calm, and her tears began to disappear. After drinking some water, she pulled her hands away. He felt bereft.

"Oh God, I'm sorry." She wiped at her wet cheeks. "I can't believe I started crying like that. I'm an idiot."

"You're not an idiot. You've been through a lot lately. I think anyone would've been scared."

She raised an eyebrow. "Would you have burst into tears after setting your oven on fire?"

"No, but I'd be pretty angry about it." He couldn't help but smile a little. "Same emotion, different reaction to it."

She sniffled. "I'm an angry crier. It's annoying. People don't take you seriously when you burst into tears because you're pissed off. Maybe I should try being like a guy. What do you do? Punch holes in walls?"

"Nothing that destructive," he said wryly. "More like swear and yell and scare away any small animals in the vicinity."

"I should try that next time."

They smiled at each other, and Caleb realized that this was the first time he'd seen Megan as really vulnerable. He'd seen her angry, aroused, amused—but he'd never once seen her cry. Not even when he'd arrested her. Any other seventeen-year-old girl would've been sobbing, but not Megan. She'd been defiant, mouthy, and a giant pain in his ass.

"Thank you," she murmured. A flush climbed up her cheeks. "You always seem to be here at my worst possible moments."

"Maybe I like you the best at your worst."

She inhaled a sharp breath. "Please, don't. I can't right now." Her voice was strained, and she wouldn't look at him.

He wanted to ask her why—why not? He wanted to ask himself that. He wished he could decipher where they stood with each other. Every day it was like the ground shifted under his feet when it came to Megan.

When she stood, he did as well, but she didn't move to leave. He couldn't help but compare this to the moment outside the Fainting Goat, how the tension had tightened until it was almost unbearable. In a gesture he knew he should regret but didn't, he brushed a smudge of soot from her silken cheek. His fingers lingered.

When she closed her eyes, he knew—she wanted him as much as he did. As much as ever. He didn't know who kissed who first. It didn't matter. He was kissing her again, and it was just as sweet as the first time—or second time. He didn't know if the first time could really count. They wrapped around each other like blooming vines, and when his tongue slicked inside her mouth, she moaned.

He murmured her name. He tasted her on his tongue, and he felt her in every limb. He wanted to consume her, take her on the desk behind her, make her his, *finally*—

"Megan, do you—Oh. Oh!"

They jumped apart like they'd been burned. When Caleb turned to see Jubilee staring at them both with wide eyes, he wanted to groan in frustration.

"You know what, never mind. I'll figure it out. I know how to use Google. Besides, you two look busy. Really busy. That's cool. Okay, bye." Jubilee scampered off, looking too amused for her own good.

Caleb swore. Megan looked like she wanted to melt into the floor. *Could they never have a moment alone without it ending awkwardly?*

"I should go," he said, because he didn't want to hear Megan say it first. "Let me know if you need any help cleaning up."

She blinked. Her lips were red and kiss-bruised, and it only made him want her more.

"Okay." Her voice was barely a whisper.

With a grunt, he stalked out of the bakery, not sure if he hated Jubilee more for interrupting them, or himself for not being able to give up on Megan Flannigan.

CHAPTER SIX

Megan felt Jubilee's gaze on her as she returned to the bakery. She refused to blush, or act like anything had happened. So what that she caught Megan kissing Caleb? It wasn't a crime. She could kiss whomever she wanted. She could kiss Caleb in her office and Jubilee couldn't say anything that would embarrass her because it wasn't a big deal.

"Jubilee, can you go finish cleaning up the kitchen for now, especially the oven? We don't want a repeat of today."

Jubilee gave her a look that spoke volumes, but since she was a smart girl, she kept her mouth shut. She did, however, give Megan an amused smile, which only made Megan scowl.

Megan served the customers for the next two hours until closing. Jubilee periodically came back to the front for something, although Megan wondered if she were just doing it to set her on edge.

I kissed Caleb. Again. It's fine. I'm not freaking out.

She told herself that over and over again, but it didn't convince her. She was freaking out. She was freaking out and she could barely concentrate on getting people baked goods and coffee without messing up. She accidentally made Maria Hepstein an iced latte instead of a hot one, and she gave Marcus Beecher a cinnamon roll instead of banana bread. She got someone's change wrong in one instance, and she almost burned herself making a basic cup of tea for someone else. By the time it was time to close, she breathed a sigh of relief. If she weren't careful, she really would burn this place down.

She rolled her eyes, mostly at herself. *Get it together, Megan,* she commanded herself. *You don't have time to mope over Caleb Thornton!*

She flipped the open sign to closed and locked the front door before going into the back. Jubilee was rolling out bread dough for tomorrow, and some of Megan's tension eased from her shoulders. Jubilee hadn't had much—if any—experience when she'd started, but she'd become indispensable to the bakery within a short time. Megan appreciated that she did tasks without having to be reminded multiple times, including rolling out dough for the morning. It was a small thing, but for some stupid reason, her throat closed up like she was going to cry.

Jubilee finished with her dough, placing a tea towel over the bowl before she put it in the fridge. Brushing her hands off, she smiled at Megan.

"Did you clean out the oven?" Megan asked, only because she didn't want Jubilee to ask her anything about Caleb.

"Yes, it's sparkling clean. I think I got most of the smoke smell out of here. What happened, anyway? You never get the oven dirty enough to smoke like that."

Megan sat on the counter, sighing. "I've been distracted. It was a stupid mistake, that's all. But it's a good reminder we should keep things in order. We can't afford something else happening here."

"True, which is why I created this checklist for us to make sure we get things like that done every day." Jubilee handed her the list attached to a clipboard.

Megan looked it over, and she smiled at the thoroughness of it. *Clean oven, wipe down counters, clean bathroom (morning, noon, evening), inventory ingredients, order supplies,* and other tasks were all in a list and grouped by type. Those pesky tears threatened again, and she had to set the list aside to brush said tears away with a brisk wipe of her hand.

Jubilee hopped up onto the counter with her. Although only four years younger than Megan, Jubilee seemed younger in many ways. It wasn't that she wasn't responsible, but she had an innocence and naiveté to her that both amused and confounded Megan. Megan knew that Jubilee had been sheltered for much of her life. She hadn't attended college or gone abroad or even lived in another town from her family like most young adults her age.

The elephant in the room only grew larger as the two women said nothing. Megan felt a blush creeping up her cheeks, and she swore inwardly.

"So…" Jubilee folded her hands in her lap. "What was that all about?"

Megan made a point to stare at the wall. "What about what?"

"Oh come on. Don't act like you don't know." Jubilee bumped Megan's shoulder. "You, my brother, *kissing*—"

Megan shushed her, even though there was no one else around. "It wasn't—no. It was just—a thing. That happened.

That won't happen again. I don't want to talk about it." Her blush only increased.

"You might not want to talk about, but I do. Not that I'm dying to know about my brother kissing anyone, you know, but considering you two act like you hate each other and then I catch you kissing…" Jubilee shrugged. "Even I can put two and two together."

"It's not going to happen again," Megan replied firmly. At Jubilee's raised eyebrow, she added, "It won't. It was a mistake. I was upset about the oven, it happened, that was it."

"You keep saying that, and yet, I don't believe you at all. I know people think that I don't know how things work, or that I've been so sheltered that I can't understand love and romance and even lust. The funny thing is that when you've been sheltered like me, it also gives you the chance to watch other people, since you haven't been allowed to live your own life. You live it through others." Jubilee played with a string that had come loose on her jeans. "And let me say that I've watched my brother—and all of my siblings—live life. And do things that I haven't. And I know Caleb well enough to know that I have never seen him look at someone the way he looks at you."

Megan's throat closed. She felt like there wasn't enough air in the room, and she covered her gasp for air with a cough.

"It doesn't matter," she said grimly. "We aren't good for each other. We never have been. There are things you don't know about, Jubi."

Jubilee shrugged again. "Maybe. But I'll just say this: if a guy looked at me the way Caleb looks at you? I wouldn't let that go so easily."

Megan didn't say anything, but only knotted her fingers in

her lap, wishing her heart didn't hurt as much as it did right then.

~

CALEB KNEW that murder was illegal, but that didn't stop him from imagining it in all its gory detail that night at the Thornton family dinner.

Family dinner had become a much smaller affair ever since Lisa, the Thornton siblings' mother, had tried to keep Harrison and his now fiancée Sara apart. Lisa had since tried to apologize to the both of them, but Harrison was still angry. Caleb couldn't blame him. Lisa had gone behind Harrison's back to convince Sara that she should give him up, and if Harrison hadn't fought like hell to get Sara back, they wouldn't be engaged.

Right now, the only Thornton siblings attending family dinner were Caleb, Jubilee, and the third eldest sibling, Mark. Mark Thornton rarely attended these dinners, as he owned and ran a ranch some one hour south of Fair Haven, and he preferred his own company for the most part. With his taciturn demeanor, dark looks, and tendency toward overt bluntness, he usually came to odds with their parents, who weren't the biggest fans of their son running a ranch. Ranches were for a different kind of people, Lisa would say, which would inevitably anger Mark and cause a fight.

Tonight, though, Lisa was on her best behavior. If Caleb didn't know better, he'd say his mother was genuinely sorry for what she'd done. She wasn't a bad person, but she had her own prejudices that she'd yet to overcome. Ironically enough, she'd been in a similar position as Sara and Harrison when she'd gone against the Thorntons to marry Dave Thornton, yet for whatever reason, the suffering she'd experienced had caused her to be more against Harrison marrying Sara.

The meal was quiet. Even Jubilee, who was normally chatty, kept quiet. Then again, she had walked in on Caleb and Megan kissing. Caleb scowled at his chicken. That entire situation was a mess, wasn't it? He kept fucking up, yet he still didn't know where he stood with Megan. He had a feeling she'd avoid him even more, which just made him groan inwardly.

"Have you seen Harrison lately?" Lisa asked in a casual voice. She cut her chicken one piece at a time, setting her knife down between each bite. "It's a shame he couldn't come tonight."

Mark grunted, which was his usual response to things. Caleb almost rolled his eyes. Jubilee decided to jump in before her brothers did.

"I saw him and Sara. They're doing great. They're talking about getting married next summer."

Lisa didn't even flinch at the mention of their marriage. "How nice. Summer is always a good time for a wedding up here in Washington."

Caleb sawed at his chicken with more gusto than necessary. He didn't know if he were more irritated at his mother for being her usual self or more frustrated with himself for not being able to avoid Megan.

"When you see Harrison again, could you please invite him to family dinner next week?" Lisa asked. "I've called him, but he won't return my calls."

"I wonder why," Caleb said wryly.

Jubilee kicked him under the table, and he grunted.

"Mark, how's the ranch?" Dave asked. "Anything new there?"

Mark drank his beer, not answering right away. He was brawnier than Harrison and Caleb, and due to his work in the sun, he was also much tanner. He had a roughness to him that tended to ruffle feathers in politer circles, which was why Mark hated the social circles that their parents were apart of. He liked his horses, and his cows, and that was about it.

Caleb had never really understood his younger brother. While Caleb and Harrison had been close growing up, Mark had been on his own for the most part. Lizzie and Seth—the twins—had had each other, and then Jubilee had had everyone wrapped around her little finger. Mark had been quiet with only a handful of friends at one time, and when he'd graduated from high school, he'd left Fair Haven without a look back. Caleb had tried to talk to Mark from time to time, but he'd gotten so busy with his own life and job that he hadn't made much of an effort lately. Seeing the dark circles underneath Mark's eyes, Caleb knew he needed to try harder to reconnect with Mark, if only to understand what was going on in his life.

"It's good. My best filly Georgia just dropped a foal, a pretty little chestnut," Mark replied, his voice low and gravelly. "I'm looking to expand into keeping goats, actually, but we'll see."

"Goats? Why goats?" Jubilee asked. "Aren't they mean?"

Mark smiled, but it was a tiny smile. A smile he only ever gave his younger sister. "They can be, but there's a huge market for goat's milk right now. I'm all about taking advantage of big markets."

"Don't they eat everything?" Caleb couldn't help but ask. "Like tin cans?"

Mark replied, "Yes. And they faint when scared."

"Sounds like fun." Caleb laughed at Lisa's expression. "Sorry, Mom. We won't keep talking about livestock at the table."

"I'd prefer that you didn't." She sniffed, her chin lifted slightly. "Mark, why don't you consider relocating here? We never see you. You're so involved with your cows and horses and pigs—"

"I don't have pigs."

"—that I'm afraid you'll lose all of your social skills." Lisa frowned. "Why do all of my children have to go away?"

Caleb opened his mouth to explain, but once again, Jubilee kicked him. He glared at her.

"Mom, Mark never had social skills," Caleb said, which just made Mark shrug in pseudo-agreement. "Wouldn't you rather he stay around his horses so he doesn't terrify people?"

"He's not that bad," Jubilee argued.

Dave just ate in silence, never one to jump into arguments unless absolutely necessary.

Once finished with dinner, the family moved to the sitting room, which Caleb thought was one of the more pretentious things his family did. At least Lisa didn't insist on the men going in first to smoke cigars and drink port, with the women following later, like some nineteenth-century novel. He sat down next to Mark, and to his great joy, Lisa settled in the chair across from them.

"Caleb, I wanted to speak with you about something," she said. "I've heard about what happened at that bakery downtown, and that you've been spending time with Sara's sister lately."

Caleb's defenses instantly went up. He gritted his teeth to keep from saying something he'd regret. Mark sensed the tension, but he only raised his eyebrows slightly. He was aware of what had happened between Harrison and Lisa, although he hadn't been witness to it.

"I just wanted to advise you to be careful. People like to talk, that's all. What with Harrison and Sara getting engaged, you now getting close to the sister…"

"Mom, I wouldn't recommend continuing with that statement," Caleb said in a low voice.

"I'm not trying to interfere." At his skeptical look, she added, "I'm not. I've learned my lesson. Just don't do anything you may regret, that's all."

He clenched his fists. He couldn't help but see the flash of judgment in Lisa's eyes, for the accident that had caused her to look at Caleb differently. How she'd pushed everything under the rug to maintain the Thorntons' status in Fair Haven. Caleb didn't know how she could think she could say anything about his relationship with Megan, but then again, Lisa never failed to do what you'd least expect.

"The only regret I have is that I'm stuck in this goddamn family." Caleb uttered the words before he realized he'd said them, but he refused to let himself feel guilty. Rising from the couch, he said tightly, "I should go. Mark, I'll call you. Jujubee, see you tomorrow."

Caleb stalked out of the house, but not before Dave followed him. His father took him by the shoulder, rather like when Caleb was a kid doing something naughty.

"You do not get to speak to your mother like that," he

said. Caleb turned to see the pain and anger on Dave's face. "She's been through enough. She just wants to help you kids, don't you see that?"

"How can you say that when she keeps hurting people?" Caleb shook his head in disgust. "I don't know how you defend her."

"Because she's my wife, and I love her. She's made mistakes—but so have I. So have we all." Dave lowered his voice. "She truly wants to make things right with Harrison, and she wants you to be happy, too. She wants all of you to be happy. Don't push her away so quickly, Caleb. She's the only mother you'll have."

Caleb didn't say anything, but only nodded tightly.

As he drove home, he got a call from the station. "This is Officer Thornton," he said automatically.

"Officer Thornton, there's been a call from 111 Third Ave S. The woman says a man followed her home, and she's afraid he's trying to get into the house."

"Copy that. Who's the woman?"

"It's Megan Flannigan."

Caleb's blood turned to ice. Turning his siren on, he raced across town, praying he would reach Megan in time.

CHAPTER SEVEN

Megan looked over her shoulder for the third time as she walked home. The hairs on the back of her neck stood on end, and she told herself she was imagining things. It didn't help that she was alone and already on edge. Walking faster, she urged her pounding heart to calm itself. *Why would somebody be following you in a place like Fair Haven?* she asked herself. This town was safety incarnate. Crime rarely happened, and Megan walked home by herself all the time.

Then again, robberies were once uncommon, until recently.

She walked faster. When she heard a rustle in a nearby shrub, she almost jumped out of her skin before seeing a skinny cat dart across the street. She inhaled a deep breath.

But the feeling that someone was following her only continued as she walked home. When she heard footsteps behind her, she whirled around, but nobody was there. She peered into a nearby yard, but she could only see the usual types of things in anybody's front yard: pots for gardening, children's toys left strewn across the grass, a kinked garden hose.

That was when she heard a noise: movement that was decidedly human in nature. Footsteps against concrete. If someone were just walking the same path as her, wouldn't she have seen that person already? She started walking faster until she practically ran all the way home. Every tree, every bush, every shadowy corner between houses seemed to be filled with threats and terrors. Although she wanted to believe she was just anxious for no reason, her gut told her otherwise.

She clutched her keys in her hand as she finally got to her front door, but her hands trembled so much that it seemed an eternity before she could unlock her door. When she burst inside and slammed the door shut, she locked the door and then proceeded to bar the door with a coffee table and chair. She didn't care if she were overreacting. Better safe than sorry, she told her panicked thoughts.

Her cat Gary sensed her anxiety, and his fur stood on end as Megan turned her house into some kind of bunker. He paced nearby before running to hide underneath the couch when Megan almost tripped over him in her haste.

"You're okay," she kept muttering to herself. "It's nothing. You were just freaking out. You're okay." Going to the living room window, she was about to pull the curtains closed when she saw somebody only feet from her window. He was dressed all in black, although she could just make out the upper half of his face underneath what looked like a black ski mask.

She screamed, and yanking the curtains closed, she ducked down to the floor. She pulled her phone from her purse to call 911, but her fingers felt like they were frozen. It took her multiple tries to punch in the right numbers, and by the time she was connected to an operator, she was close to sobbing.

"A man followed me home," she gasped out. "I just saw him outside my window."

The operator asked for her name and address in a calm voice before confirming what Megan had seen.

"An officer is on his way, ma'am," the woman said. "But call back if you see anything else or the situation escalates."

"Okay. Okay." Megan pressed a hand to her pounding heart, terror making her almost dizzy. "How far away is the officer?"

"He'll be there in five minutes. I'll stay on the line with you until he arrives."

Those five minutes felt like hours, days, years, as the operator kept her panic at bay. But when Megan heard the knock on her front door, she almost jumped out of her skin. She cowered underneath her window, unable to move.

"Megan, it's me, Caleb," Caleb called through the door. "Are you okay? Megan, are you in there?"

"The officer is here," she told the operator as she slowly got to her feet.

"Please confirm that it is Officer Thornton," the operator replied.

She cracked the door open, and when she saw his face, relief made her dizzy. "Caleb. Oh my God." She spoke into her phone, "It's Officer Thornton. Thank you for your help." After hanging up, she couldn't find the words to thank Caleb for coming.

He didn't move to get her to open the door further, instead speaking in that calm, capable voice that she knew he used when he was on duty. "I'm going to case the perimeter of your house. Stay inside."

She locked the front door and sat down on the couch only yards away, her hands clenched into fists. Gary eventually emerged from under the couch to sit beside her, and she petted his fur to soothe her nerves.

She didn't jump when Caleb knocked again, but it did set her heart pounding once again. He called out her name, confirming it was him.

This time, she opened the door fully to let him inside.

"It's all clear," he said, but he didn't move to come inside. "The perp probably disappeared the second he realized that you'd seen him." His voice gentled as he asked, "May I come inside? I need to take your statement."

She nodded, her mind barely working at this point. She found herself sitting on her couch with Caleb sitting in an armchair adjacent, and she answered his questions as best she could. He was patient yet thorough, and she recounted what she'd seen as best she could.

Gary climbed into her lap, which helped her anxiety a little. After he'd gotten what he'd needed, Caleb frowned down at his notepad.

"What is it?" Megan asked. She petted Gary too hard, which earned her a brief swat and a swishing tail.

"Only that more than likely, this is connected to your bakery's robbery, although I don't have a motive to go off of." He sounded frustrated. "Are you sure there isn't anyone who would consider you an enemy? Someone that would be angry with you?"

She couldn't help but laugh, but it came out more like a

sob. "The only person I seem to piss of regularly is sitting in front of me."

That earned her a small smile. "I'll call this into the station, especially to make sure there haven't been any other incidents that are similar lately."

He left to make his call, and Megan found herself unable to figure out what she should do. For some reason, the basics had fled her mind. She realized that she hadn't even turned on a light, and that the only light was coming from the streetlamps outside. Moving Gary off of her lap, she flipped on a lamp before sitting back down. Should she call somebody? Sara? Her mom? She didn't want to call anyone—except Caleb.

She hadn't known how much she'd wanted him to be the officer that arrived until she'd seen him at her door. His presence reassured her like no one else's would. He would keep her safe without adding to her anxiety like her sister would. Sara would try to cosset and bundle her up in metaphorical wool until Megan couldn't breathe. Caleb, though, treated the situation with a calmness that Megan had needed.

"Okay, that's done," Caleb said as he returned. "The next question is: do you have any place to stay tonight? I would rather you didn't stay here alone tonight. Can you stay with your sister?"

Megan clutched a throw pillow as she shook her head. "I don't want to bother her."

"A friend? Your mom?"

She just kept shaking her head. "I don't want to stay with anyone else. I don't want people to make a big deal out of this." For some stupid reason, she felt embarrassed. For whatever reason, life had decided to hand her a bad deal, but the last thing she wanted was anyone to pity her. If Megan despised anything, it was pity.

Caleb let out a sigh. "Obviously I'm not going to force you to call anyone, but you staying here by yourself is not a good idea. This guy isn't going to stop, and once he sees that you're by yourself again, he'll use that to his advantage. Besides, looking at this house, it would be easy for an intruder to get inside."

Her eyes widened. "What?"

He seemed to regret that he'd said anything, but he admitted, "The window at the back of the house? It was unlocked. Since you're at ground level, it would be easy to cut the screen and climb through. The backdoor, too. You could break the glass, unlock the door, and get inside in seconds."

"That's…terrible." She clutched the pillow harder. Gary hopped up next to her again and began to knead her thigh. "How did I never think of that before?"

"Because you shouldn't have to. This is usually a safe town. That being said, it isn't right now for you. So if you aren't willing to stay with someone, I'll stay here tonight with you instead."

She stilled. Staring at Caleb—his expression completely serious—she couldn't believe he'd stay here. In her house. At night. Like some kind of…boyfriend.

Her throat closed.

"No, no, you don't have to—that's not necessary. I'll be fine. I'll lock the window, and I'll even lock my bedroom door. That guy is long gone." She didn't even know what she was saying, but she knew one thing: she couldn't have Caleb in her house. He was already too close in every other sense. Having him sitting on her couch or using her kitchen or, even worse, going into her bedroom?

"I'll sleep on your couch." He moved to touch the back of her hand. "It's no trouble. Really. But I'm not going to leave you alone like this."

She realized with a start that he wasn't wearing his police uniform, which meant he wasn't technically on duty. He'd taken the call when he didn't have to. Her heart flip-flopped in her chest.

How could she ever escape Caleb Thornton when he did things like this?

"Okay," she murmured. "Fine. You can stay. Let me go get blankets and pillows..." She looked at his outfit—jeans and a sweater—and asked, "And maybe something to wear? Although I don't have any men's clothes here..."

He grinned. "It's fine. I won't be sleeping anyway."

That admission didn't help her nerves one bit. She wouldn't be sleeping tonight either, not with Caleb only feet away in her living room. She hurried away into the hall closet to pull out a stack of blankets and pillows and even a towel and washcloth, in case he wanted to shower. Frozen, she couldn't stop the image of Caleb, showering, *naked*, from appearing in her head.

This is the worst idea of all time, she thought frantically. She tossed the towel and washcloth back into the closet before she could think about Caleb being naked anymore.

I'm losing my mind. Completely losing it. Somebody check me into the asylum because apparently I can only make very poor life choices. She almost burst out laughing, but she covered her mouth before the sound emerged.

She handed Caleb the blankets and pillows once she'd

found some modicum of calm. To her amusement, her absence had resulted in Gary deciding that Caleb was his newest lap to sit on.

"What kind of cat is this?" Caleb asked as Gary proceeded to knead his leg. He winced when the cat got a little too close to his crotch for comfort. "And why is he torturing me like this?"

Megan smiled for the first time in what felt like ages. "Have you never had a cat before? No? Well, they do that when they feel safe. When they're kittens they knead their mothers when they're nursing. It's something leftover from babyhood, I guess."

"Huh." Gary finally turned in multiple circles before settling onto Caleb's lap. "Why is his face weird like that?"

"His face is beautiful!" She bent down to pet Gary behind his silken ears. A rumbling purr began to emerge from his small body. "Don't listen to him, Gary. It's his face that's weird."

"Is it? I'll have to take that up with my parents."

Megan looked up, only to realize that she was inches from Caleb and that at this angle, he could look down her shirt with ease. She blushed and lurched away.

She saw his green eyes twinkle, his mouth twisting into a small smile.

"Well, I'm going to get ready for bed." She looked at the clock on the wall. "Even if it's only nine o'clock. Um, do you need anything else?"

"I'm good." He petted Gary with slow strokes.

She couldn't stop herself from wishing she were that cat, which only increased her discomfort. Before she could do something really stupid, she hurried from the room.

CHAPTER EIGHT

Caleb heard the water turn on in Megan's bathroom, and he almost groaned aloud. Was she taking a bath? A shower? Either way, she'd be naked, and only a room away. He gritted his teeth as the inevitable images of her wet, naked, and flushed from the heat of her bath filled his mind.

"Don't do this right now," he muttered to himself. Gary swiveled his ears at the sound, especially when Caleb stopped petting him. He continued the petting, mostly because he wasn't sure the cat wouldn't get its revenge on his balls if he did something it didn't like.

He hadn't told Megan he was staying here just so he could be a creep. This was what he told himself, but he knew that deep down, he'd wanted to be the one to stay here. To protect her from the threat outside, and, yes, to just be in the same place as her. It was like a sickness. He'd already kissed her this week, and now he was going to be on her couch all night while she lay in her own bed. What did she wear to bed? Pajamas? Lingerie? Nothing?

Get ahold of yourself, he told himself. *You're here to keep her safe and nothing else.*

His mind knew what he should be doing, but his body wanted something else entirely.

He turned on the TV, but even some drama couldn't keep him occupied. He only took in Megan's house—a small but well-maintained one-story bungalow that exuded a warmth that Caleb had never felt at his own childhood home. The furniture wasn't brand-new, the TV was a few years old, and the carpet was rather worn, but it was somehow better than the glittering coldness of his parents' living room. Caleb took in the framed photos on the wall, the romance novels scattered across the coffee table, the smell of cinnamon and lemon that permeated the air. It was homey, he decided. Comfortable.

The bright blue bookshelf, filled with various cookbooks and novels, drew his gaze. He realized the entire space was colorful, and it seemed to be exactly as he would've imagined Megan Flannigan's house: bright and well-loved.

When she emerged from the bathroom, her hair wet, with her wearing nothing but a tank top and short pajama bottoms, Caleb couldn't stop himself from turning into some kind of hunting dog, suddenly on point and on alert. She was beautiful, her skin creamy, her red hair piled on top of her head in a messy bun. He drank her in, from the curve of her neck to the bright purple polish on her toes.

He swallowed against a suddenly dry throat.

"Oh good, you found the remote. You want anything to eat? Drink? I'm hungry now for some reason. I guess being terrified brings out your appetite?" she babbled, and Caleb found it so charming. The only reason he didn't take her into his arms and kiss her was because he still had a cat on his lap.

Oh, and it would be a terrible idea, because he and Megan could never be what he would want them to be.

"I'm fine," he said.

She blinked at his terseness. "Okay, well, holler if you need anything."

He listened to her putter around in the kitchen. The smell of cheese filled the air, and his mouth watered. He'd barely eaten anything at the Thornton family dinner that night, and he hadn't realized how hungry he was until now. Gently moving Gary onto the couch cushion beside him—Gary glared but decided to give himself a bath right then—Caleb followed Megan into the kitchen.

He leaned against the doorframe and watched her: she flipped a quesadilla over before taking a whistling kettle off the stove. If he let himself, he could imagine watching her do this all the time, like they were together. His heart did that obnoxious flip flop inside his chest, but he couldn't stop himself from imagining what it would be like to be with her. Would she cook for him? Or would she tell him to fend for himself? He grinned at that. Megan wouldn't coddle anyone —except maybe the cat currently licking itself on her couch.

When she went to a nearby cabinet, she finally noticed him standing there. Jumping a little, she dropped the box of teabags she'd just pulled down. Caleb went to her and picked up the box the same moment she bent down to retrieve them.

"Didn't mean to scare you," he mumbled. They both stood, their gazes locked on each other. The hairs on Caleb's arms rose, and the tension became unbearably thick. When he placed the box in her palm, he couldn't stop himself from brushing his fingers against her hand before drawing away.

"It's okay. Are you hungry? Or do you want some tea?"

She looked away and put distance between them, and Caleb felt the space like a hole in his chest.

"You have anything stronger than tea?" he asked.

At that, she paled a little, and she wouldn't look at him. "I don't keep alcohol in the house," was all she said. She flipped off the stove and placed her quesadilla on a plate, her movements jerky, like she was distracted.

Caleb instantly cursed himself. *Good job, jackass.* She'd gotten arrested for public intoxication, and her mother had suffered from alcoholism, so it stood to reason Megan would forgo drinking altogether. *She's a better person than I am,* he thought morosely.

"Sorry," was all he said. "Tea would be great. Where are the cups?"

She pointed to a cabinet to his right. Pulling down two mugs, he poured the hot water from the kettle and added teabags to both. He almost commented that a quesadilla and tea seemed like an odd combination to him, but he found it so completely Megan-like that it made him smile.

When his stomach growled, Megan looked up from the mug of tea she was sipping. "You sure about not being hungry?"

"I could eat," he admitted, "but I'll make something for myself."

She shrugged. "Suit yourself. There's ramen in the pantry. Not sure I trust you to cook anything more complicated than that."

That did elicit a grin from him, and before he knew it, they were in the living room eating their meals and watching TV, Gary the cat settled between them. They didn't talk, but they didn't need to. Caleb had never felt this comfortable in anyone's house before. It was a strange sensation, he had to admit, sitting in Megan's living room and drinking tea and watching late-night talk shows.

Before long, though, Megan began to drift off, and he took her mug from her hand to set it on the coffee table. Gathering her into his arms, he carried her to bed, settling her underneath the covers. She curled into a little ball, and Caleb couldn't stop himself from kissing her on the forehead before he left.

MEGAN HEARD A CRASH, which jolted her awake. It took her a moment to realize she was in her own bed, with the lights off. Had she gone to bed? The last thing she remembered was Caleb taking her mug of tea from her hand while they'd been sitting on the couch together.

Her heart raced as she listened. Eventually, she let out the breath she'd been holding. *It was just a dream. I was dreaming and something crashed in my dream.* But as she reassured herself with those words, she knew she wasn't going to fall asleep again. She stared up at the ceiling, trying not to listen for movement in the living room. Was Caleb asleep? Or was he staring up at the ceiling just like she was?

She also realized that her nightly feline companion wasn't curled up next to her like he always was. With a frown, she got out of bed to search for Gary. She tiptoed into the living room. The TV was still on, providing a measure of light, and she saw that Caleb was reclined on the couch with Gary on his chest, his tail swishing.

Caleb saw her and was about to sit up, but she shook her head.

"I was looking for Gary," she explained. A blush climbed up her cheeks as she realized how lame of an excuse that was. "He always sleeps with me."

Gary's ears twitched at the sound of her voice, but he didn't awaken. Stretching out a leg, he almost swiped Caleb on the chin as he extended his claws.

"Apparently he's my new best friend." Caleb's voice was wry, but he didn't move to shoo the cat away. Instead, he gently picked up Gary as he sat up, placing the cat in his lap. Gary was in such a deep sleep that he didn't even notice the chest-to-lap transfer.

Megan's mouth twitched from trying not to laugh.

"Couldn't sleep?" Caleb's voice was low, concerned. Megan couldn't stop herself from sitting down next to him, even though a small voice inside her head warned that she should go back to her bedroom and lock her door for good measure.

Not because she was afraid of Caleb. She was afraid of herself.

"I heard a noise, but I was dreaming. You couldn't sleep either?"

He shrugged. "I don't need a lot of sleep. What were you dreaming about?"

She hesitated, not sure she should say anything. Telling him about this would be another form of intimacy, and hadn't she told herself that that would be a terrible idea?

But more and more, she wanted to believe she and Caleb wouldn't be a terrible idea. She'd avoided him when she'd believed he wasn't interested in her. Things had changed—at least, she hoped things had changed. His interest in her had certainly shifted since he'd set her aside when she'd been all of seventeen. Was it so foolish to hope now?

"I can't remember exactly, but the man was chasing me. I couldn't move. You know those dreams where you want to run or scream, yet you can't? It was one of those. He kept getting closer and closer and I wanted to yell for help. I couldn't do anything. I was just stuck." She shivered. "I hate those dreams. Then I heard what I thought was a crash, but when I woke up, I realized I was dreaming. I guess I dreamed that he crashed into me?"

Caleb considered her. She could just make out his expression with the bright light of the TV backlighting him.

"We'll find this guy, Megan. I can promise you that." His voice was low, consoling, and when he touched her hand, she didn't pull away. "He'll fuck up, and we'll catch him."

"What if he does something worse next time? And you're not there? You can't be with me twenty-four-seven, Caleb." Her voice trembled, and she hated herself for it. When did she become so weak? What had happened to the Megan who could take care of herself?

"I won't let that happen. If I have to sleep on your couch for the next month, I will," he vowed. He squeezed her fingers, and she squeezed back. "I'll never let anything or anyone hurt you. I already lost one friend..." His voice trailed away, and he pulled his hand from hers.

She felt bereft—and curious. Who had he lost?

"Do you think of me as a friend?" she couldn't help but ask.

His lips quirked upward. "A friend who drives me crazy? Yes. I know we haven't always been our best around each other, but I hope you consider us friends. In some twisted way."

She wished the butterflies in her stomach hadn't started to flutter quite so madly at his statement. *He considers you a friend and nothing more*, she cautioned herself, but it didn't matter. This was a step in the right direction. If he thought of her as a friend, that meant he cared about her, and if he cared about her…

"Thank you." She rubbed her arms, and those butterflies only fluttered more when Caleb wrapped a blanket around her. "Thank you, for a second time," she said with a little laugh.

Maybe it was the darkness, or the time of night, or the feeling of safety sitting next to this man who'd just vowed to keep her shadows at bay. Maybe it was that no matter how hard a person tried to keep everything locked inside, inevitably, the need to share, to confide, overpowered those protective walls around one's heart. Or maybe it was that Megan felt a cord of communion between herself and Caleb, and with every breath and beat of her heart, it only strengthened between them

"When I was a kid, I didn't always feel safe," she admitted. "You know about my mom…"

He nodded, but he didn't say anything.

She inhaled a breath. "Well, when she drank, Sara and I didn't have a parent. Our mom was passed out drunk on the couch or at some bar, and we had to fend for ourselves. Sara did her best—she ended up being the mom our own mom wasn't. She went to the grocery store, she went to Goodwill to get me clothes for school." A sad smile touched Megan's lips. "She tried her hardest, but she was a kid, too. But for so many years, I would lie awake at night and listen for my mom to come home, hoping that she would and also hoping she wouldn't come back. I was terrified that a police officer would come knocking to tell us she was in the hospital or, worse, dead." She swallowed against the sudden tightness in her throat. "It was hard to concentrate in school. I couldn't invite friends over. Sometimes I would get so scared that I couldn't breathe.

"I don't want to feel like that ever again," she said as she caught Caleb's gaze. "I don't want to feel helpless. I vowed to myself I would never be in that position again. I hate that this person has made me feel like this again, like a little girl who can't do a damn thing for herself."

Tears spilled over, but she wiped them away with a brusque gesture. She refused to cry in front of Caleb—again. *I can't be weak. I can't break down.* She swallowed until the tears seemed to disappear, her sniffling the only sound in the darkened room.

When Caleb didn't say anything, she let out an awkward laugh. It was a cross between a giggle and a sob, and she was infinitely glad the room was dark enough that he couldn't see how badly she was blushing right now.

"God, I'm a mess," she muttered as she started to get off the couch. "I should try to get some sleep."

"No, don't. Stay." He touched her arm.

She gazed down at him. Her heart thumped, and she was surprised he couldn't hear it as well. The movement also jostled Gary enough to awaken him. Hopping down from Caleb's lap with a yowl of annoyance, he hopped onto the nearby chair to sleep un-accosted.

"You've lost me my cat, so now you definitely have to

stay." His voice curled around her body like tendrils of silk. "So you owe me."

She sat down, smiling a little. "I'm not sure how that logic works, but okay. I wouldn't want you to get bored."

"Around you, Megan, I'm never, ever bored."

Memories of their kiss—the first one, the second one, the third one—filled her mind. Heat licked at her limbs, and her blood rushed through her veins.

She didn't know who moved first. She only knew that Caleb had his hand on her cheek and she had her hand on his thigh, and then their mouths met in what felt like a sort of inevitability.

His lips were soft but insistent, and she gladly opened to him. She moaned breathily as he kissed her—kissed her so thoroughly that her body was practically melting—and he hauled her onto his lap. Her legs around his hips, she couldn't help but notice the hardness pulsing against her. She shivered in his arms.

At least I know that he still wants me. The thought thrilled her, and she kissed him harder.

He sifted his fingers through her hair, and the messy bun she'd put it in earlier collapsed. He wrapped tendrils of it around his fingers as he licked inside her mouth. The bristle on his chin and cheeks rasped her skin. Humming delightedly, she threw herself into the kiss, not caring that this would probably end badly, that he hadn't come here to kiss her but to do his job, that Caleb Thornton was like a drug she'd never gotten out of her system.

No, she didn't think about any of those things.

He broke their kiss, but only so he could kiss down her throat. She felt the warm silk of his tongue laving a trail, and she tipped her head back to give him better access. When he nipped her, she gasped. Her breasts ached, and her nipples peaked under the thin cotton of her tank top. She wasn't wearing a bra, and when Caleb cupped one breast in his palm and realized this fact, he let out a tortured groan.

"God, you drive me insane. Why couldn't you wear oversized long underwear or something?" He sounded deeply disgruntled by this.

She laughed. "Because it's summer and I don't own any?" She pushed against his palm, and the sensation of his warm hand on her breast made her shiver. "Touch me, Caleb. Please."

He grunted, which she took as assent. He pulled the straps of her tank down her arms to expose her breasts. She couldn't see his expression well in the dark, but she couldn't help but tremble as he stared at her, like he couldn't believe this was happening.

She couldn't believe this was happening, either, yet it also felt *right*. She wanted this. She wanted him.

His thumb brushed over one tightened peak. It was barely a touch, but she felt it through every nerve of her body. She panted as he thumbed one nipple and then the other, rubbing them until they were aching buds, desperate for his attention.

He kissed her on her sternum. "Fuck, you smell good," he rumbled. "I wish I could see these beauties better, though, but I'm sure as hell not getting up off this couch."

She grinned, running her hands down his broad shoulders, feeling the tight muscles of his arms. What would Caleb look like without a shirt on? Magnificent, she decided. He had a lean strength, almost wiry, but deeply masculine. She ran her hands over his chest, feeling his heart thumping beneath the fabric of his sweater.

When he tipped her backward onto the couch, she let out a squeal of surprise. He kissed her like a marauder, taking complete control, and she loved it. She'd had more than one boyfriend in her past, and sex had always been enjoyable. Some guys were better than others. But she'd never liked having any guy try to take over, mostly because that meant they would get their pleasure while neglecting her own.

But with Caleb, she knew that wouldn't be the case. As he scattered kisses along her collarbone before circling a nipple with the tip of his tongue, she didn't move to stop him. She only arched toward his mouth, begging for more.

He sucked one nipple, muttering her name, and she touched his hair. When he stripped her of her pajama shorts and panties, she only let out a moan. She was desperate for his touch, for release, and as he played with her breasts while his long fingers sifted through the curls covering her sex, she thought she might die if he didn't go faster.

She tugged on his hair, which made him nip her below her left breast. He moved down until his face was right above her sex, and he watched her in the darkness as he parted her folds and petted her. She knew she was wet already, and his light strokes only made her wetter. She felt swollen; she pulsed against his fingers. She didn't even realize she was begging for more until she heard a voice, seemingly distant, in her ears.

"You're so gorgeous." He dipped a finger into her sheath, and she clenched around the invasion. "I'm going to make you come so hard that you'll never think of any man but me. Every time you touch yourself here, you'll think of me."

Her eyes widened, but she only undulated faster as he pressed a second finger inside of her. "Caleb…"

"Because you're mine, Megan. Mine, and mine only. You know it and I know it. Say it. Say you're mine."

She gasped. She bit her hand to stop from screaming, and then she cursed when he withdrew his hand.

"I'm yours," she whispered. It felt like a vow.

"God, baby." He kissed her on her sex, his tongue delving through her folds, and she lost her mind.

Pressing her legs apart so he could rest between them, Caleb laved her sex, the sound of his licks and groans of appreciation mingling with her own desperate sounds. She was so close already. He thrust his fingers inside her again, and when he sucked her clit inside his mouth, she exploded. Like powder to match, she detonated, and she shook so hard that the couch shook underneath her.

Caleb continued to kiss and lick and suck, drawing her orgasm out as long as he could. She gasped for air, and she felt like she'd died. Euphoria and terror took over in equal measures within her heart.

Caleb drew her up and into his arms, and she clung to him like a sailor lost at sea.

I think I'm in love with him was the last thought in her head before she fell into a blissfully dreamless sleep.

CHAPTER NINE

The morning following their night together, Megan struggled to stay focused in the bakery. She was infinitely thankful that Jubilee had the day off, otherwise she knew the girl would interrogate her mercilessly about her brother staying the night. Not that Megan would've volunteered that information, but nothing in Fair Haven stayed a secret longer than maybe one day, if not two, if you were lucky.

Megan glanced outside to where Caleb stood on patrol. Her body heated—only from looking at his back!—and memories assailed her with such thoroughness that she didn't hear the customer clearing his throat the first time. Or the second time.

"Ma'am," the man said. "You okay?"

She almost dropped the pastry in her hand, and a bright blush bloomed on her cheeks. Flustered, she muttered, "I'm fine. Sorry. Here's your Danish."

The man nodded slowly. "Great. How about that coffee, too?"

Megan restrained herself from hitting her forehead against the counter. *Get it together!*

Although she continued to peer at Caleb from the corner of her eye all morning, she was busy enough that she was able to convince herself that she wasn't bothered by his presence. Or that she wasn't thinking of how he kissed her last night. Or how he said her name, or how warm and solid he'd felt, or how he'd smiled that smile that could melt any girl's panties when they'd awoken in the early hours of the morning. Or how he'd made her scrambled eggs that were burnt and tasteless and yet they'd somehow managed to be the best eggs she'd ever eaten.

By lunchtime, her nerves were slightly more settled. After cleaning the tables in the front, she heard the front door bell ring.

"Welcome!" she called over her shoulder. "I'll be with you in a minute."

Megan wiped the last of the crumbs and headed to the register. She smiled with genuine happiness when she saw who it was: Abby Davison, a nurse at the local hospital in Fair Haven. Short and plump with light brown hair, Abby exuded a warmth that Megan rather envied. Abby understood people, and she was the type of woman you could confide in after meeting her only recently. When she saw Megan, her lips curved into a smile.

Abby wasn't traditionally pretty, but she had a fresh-faced kind of beauty, with her bright complexion and dark-lashed brown eyes. As far as Megan knew, Abby was single, and the wheels in her mind started to turn.

Just because I can't get my love life together doesn't mean I can't help other people's, right?

"Abby, so nice to see you," Megan said. "How are you? It's been a while."

"I know, I'm sorry. It's been crazy at work, but today I woke up craving one of your cinnamon rolls. Can I get one of those and an Americano?"

"Of course. Coming right up."

As Megan made Abby's coffee, she asked, "How's work? Last time we talked, you were looking at a promotion."

"That's right. I got the promotion. I'm the head nurse in the ER, which basically means I get to tell every other nurse what to do while I get to go to boring meetings with adminis-trators."

Megan laughed. "Sounds fun. So I guess you don't have to empty bed pans or do sponge baths?"

"No, thankfully. Those things are for the LPNs."

Megan handed Abby her coffee and, after Abby had paid, they chatted for a bit longer. Megan realized with an inner grimace that she really should've messaged Abby earlier about getting lunch or coffee. She'd been so wrapped up in work that she'd neglected friendships as a result.

Abby cocked her head, gesturing at Caleb standing outside. "I heard about what happened. How's it going? And with that guy hanging around all day?"

Megan considered, but she needed to confide in someone. Sara was too busy with Harrison and James, and Megan didn't want to upset her. So Megan told Abby everything—the man following her, Caleb staying over. Well, except for the heavy petting on her couch. Some things a girl needed to keep to herself.

Despite the fact that Megan didn't say anything about what had happened on her couch, Abby sensed there was more to the story. "I wouldn't blame any woman going after him, even if he is a Thornton. He's yummy in that uniform. And everybody knows that he's had a thing for you since the dawn of time."

"He has not," Megan said automatically. Because if she denied it out loud, then she wouldn't obsess over him. Or something. Her mind was so twisted up that sometimes she didn't know what was up or what was down.

"Yes, he has. You know he has. Don't act like you don't know. I know you think you guys have this hatred for one another or something, but it's all foreplay." Abby sipped her coffee while pinching bites of cinnamon roll to pop into her mouth. "You should get on that, otherwise somebody else will."

"What, like you?" Megan almost growled.

Abby laughed, a bright sound that filled the bakery. "No, not me, only because you'll murder me in my sleep. I like being alive, thank you very much. Besides, I'm tired of men. I'm on a man-Sabbatical."

Megan knew vaguely that Abby had had a boyfriend, but nothing about the particulars. She almost asked her what had happened, when the front door bell rang and in walked not just one, but three Thornton men: Harrison, Caleb, and another brother who Megan had only seen a handful of times. Mark Thornton? She thought that was his name.

Seeing that trio of pure testosterone entering her bakery rather felt like her world tilting on its axis. It was no wonder the men were popular with the opposite sex: with their good looks and sex appeal, they were a sight to behold. Yet only one Thornton drew Megan's eyes: Caleb, whose dark-green-eyed gaze held her own until she was rather afraid flames were licking up and down her body.

Her attention was only diverted when she saw the look in Mark's eyes when he looked at Abby. Megan knew when a man was interested, and Mark's eyes seemed to spark with it as he took in the pretty nurse.

"Ladies," Harrison drawled, his handsome face creasing into a smile. "Megan, I don't believe I know your friend."

Thankful for the respite from Caleb, who looked apt to carry Megan outside and lock her up in his tower, Megan replied, "This is Abby Davison. She works at Fair Haven Memorial."

Abby shook hands with Caleb and Harrison, yet Mark stood behind, his hands in his back pockets.

"Have you met our younger brother?" Caleb asked. "This is Mark. He only comes to civilization twice a year. Or is it just a once a year now?"

Mark's lips curled. "I try not to leave my ranch more than I need to."

"You own a ranch?" Abby asked.

"In Milltown. Ever heard of it? No? Most people haven't. It's a dot on the map. Most people drive past it on their way to Portland."

"I have heard of Milltown, actually." To Megan's surprise, Abby seemed…flustered, but only if you paid attention. Otherwise, her aplomb was remarkable, and Megan attributed it to her working in a fast-pace environment like the ER.

"Maybe I should visit your ranch on my next trip to Portland," Abby said. "What do you do? Raise cows? Horses? Chickens?"

Mark snorted. "For one, the ranch is no place for a

woman." He slowly took her in, his gaze traveling from her toes, lingering on her breasts, and then her face. "Secondly, I raise horses."

"And pigs. Right, bro?" Caleb teased.

This seemed to be an ongoing joke between the two, and Megan rather expected them to start wrestling like young boys right in the middle of her bakery. Harrison just slapped Mark on the shoulder.

"How about we get something to eat and not keep bothering these ladies?" Harrison winked at Megan. "Otherwise I think they're going to kick us out."

After serving the Thornton trio, Megan headed to the kitchen to get another sheet of cinnamon rolls to place inside the bakery's case. She didn't hear the footsteps following her until she felt an arm snake around her waist.

She didn't have to look behind her to know who it was.

"I've wanted to kiss you all morning," Caleb rumbled. He kissed the back of her neck, and she shivered in his arms.

"I'm holding a tray," she said lamely, like it would somehow keep him from kissing her. She was sure she could feel his smile against her skin.

"Then I'll kiss you here," he said as he kissed her nape. "And here," he murmured, kissing her ear. "And here." The last kiss was on the corner of her mouth.

"Caleb, someone will see us."

"So? They've already seen us." He cupped her breast, and she had to bite her lip to stifle a moan. "Go out with me tonight."

She couldn't think with him thumbing her nipple, and she couldn't think as he kissed and suckled her neck. She tightened her grip on the tray of cinnamon rolls.

"Why?" It was the only thing that came to mind.

"Why not? Besides, you owe me for staying over last night."

At that, she swiveled her head to look him in the eye. "I didn't know there was a payment plan involved."

"There is now, only because I know you would hate to owe me anything." His fingers inched up her shirt, touching bare skin. "Go out with me tonight, or I'll ravish you on the counter right here."

Her eyes widened. "You wouldn't." Yet his fingers only moved higher and higher until he was cupping her breast underneath her bra. She closed her eyes.

"I would, and you know I would." He whispered in her ear, "Go out to dinner with me, and then I'll take you home, and I'll make love to you all night long." Rolling her nipple between his index finger and thumb, he was relentless. "Or I won't stop right now."

When Megan heard a noise, she almost jumped out of her skin. Caleb steadied the tray before she could drop it, and she set it down on the counter with a clatter. Just as she was pulling her bra back into place and her shirt over her belly, Harrison walked into the kitchen.

Caleb just raised an eyebrow.

"Fine, I'll go," she hissed. She didn't know why she was so annoyed. She had a feeling she was just frustrated with him for stoking the flames of her desire and then leaving her hanging. If he wanted to, he could touch her and she'd come under his fingers within seconds.

How humiliating. And disastrous. *Oh, and amazing, damn him.*

"I need to get back to work," Harrison said. He made a

point not to look at Megan, but she knew he knew that they'd not only been talking back here. Her face flamed. "You coming?" Harrison asked Caleb.

"Yeah, I'll be right there."

Harrison raised a dark eyebrow at his brother before nodding at Megan.

Alone again, Caleb drew Megan into his arms. "I'll pick you up at seven."

"Is that so? Not six? Seven-thirty? It has to be seven?"

"It has to be seven." He kissed her forehead. "Be a good girl and be ready for me when I come."

"Oh, I'm always ready for when you come," she drawled.

Caleb guffawed, pinching her on the ass in revenge.

"I THOUGHT you had to get back to work," Caleb said as he sat down at the table Harrison and Mark currently occupied. In a semi-private corner, he could almost act like Megan wasn't only yards away in her kitchen, looking deliciously rumpled after his kisses.

Sure, he could totally act like that wasn't a reality right now. Too bad his aching cock told him otherwise.

"I lied." Harrison tossed a bite of muffin into his mouth. "I just thought you'd rather avoid getting caught with your pants down. Again."

Caleb grunted and gave Harrison the finger. "I haven't gotten caught with my pants down ever," he muttered.

"Metaphorically. Jubilee told me all about what happened the day before. And then a little bird told me that you stayed over at Megan Flannigan's last night." Harrison grinned at

Caleb's stormy expression. "So that would be a yes, you did stay over."

"Since when did you become a gossiping old woman?" Mark said in his gravelly voice. "You're worse than Mom."

All three brothers stared at each other and then shuddered. No one was worse than Lisa Thornton when interfering in her children's lives. The thought of becoming like her was as terrifying as going outside without pants on, or an alien invasion, or nuclear war. *All three combined would still not be as bad*, Caleb thought with another inward shudder.

"I'm not going to go behind his back, so this is different. Take it from someone who's going to marry the love of his life" —Caleb and Mark groaned simultaneously— "and let me say that you shouldn't waste any more time, Caleb. You'll regret it. Get that woman and make her yours."

"Either shit or get off the pot," Mark offered.

"Exactly. Except maybe keep that sentiment to yourself."

Caleb rolled his eyes. "If it'll shut up you two busybodies, we're going out tonight. On a real, honest-to-goodness date. If you want to tag along and give me tips, feel free. Maybe you can sit behind us and whisper what I should say into my ear."

"Hey, I don't give a shit whether you shit or not." Mark finished his coffee in a single gulp. "I don't have a horse in this race."

"Enough with the metaphors." Harrison pointed a finger at Caleb. "You're really taking her out?"

"Yes, and then I'm taking her back to my place to have my way with her. You happy?"

"Deliriously." Harrison lowered his voice as he added, "But if you hurt her, I'll have to kill you. She's my sister now, too."

"She isn't your sister yet, and shouldn't you be worried she'll kill me?"

Mark grunted again. "He has a point."

"Thank you, Mark." Caleb scratched his jaw. "I think."

Harrison shook his head. "Megan puts on a brave face, but she's vulnerable if you look below the surface. Don't break her, Caleb. Because one false move could shatter her."

Caleb just scowled. For one, since when was his older brother a shrink? Last time he checked was a damn pediatric oncologist. But ever since he'd gotten engaged to Sara, Harrison felt like he needed to give everyone advice. Secondly, Caleb knew that Megan wasn't that fragile. She had a strength and starch to her spine that he'd never encountered before in another woman.

Maybe it just means that you have the power to shatter someone like her, his mind whispered.

That only soured his mood further, and he couldn't help but wonder if he was making a huge mistake. Hadn't he told himself Megan was off limits to him? That made him a fraud and a liar. A man who had secrets that he couldn't reveal to anyone. A man who'd caused the death of his best friend and had never received any punishment for it.

Right then, Megan's friend Abby walked by, her phone glued to her ear. Caleb had seen her around town a number of times although he'd never talked to her. She was pretty, although nothing about her screamed beauty queen. Wearing scrubs and her hair in a tight bun, she blended easily into the crowd. Yet Caleb couldn't help but notice that Mark seemed to vibrate with tension when she passed by.

Now, that was interesting.

Mark had had a fiancée once upon a time, but it had

ended badly. Caleb wasn't sure of all of the details—Mark wasn't exactly a chatty guy—but at the end of everything, Mark's fiancée had suddenly become Mark's best friend's girl-friend. Ever since then, Mark had had a dark cloud over him, a bitterness that no woman had been able to penetrate. Caleb had honestly wondered if Mark would remain a monk forever.

Based on his reaction to Abby, his stint with celibacy might be at an end.

Abby walked away, probably to a table in the back of the bakery.

Harrison also noticed the look in Mark's eyes and said casually, "Why don't you ask her out?"

Mark seemed to jolt out of whatever reverie he'd been under. "What? Who?"

"Abby, of course."

Mark scowled. "Don't play matchmaker with me. I'm not interested in dating any woman."

That raised the eyebrows of both Harrison and Caleb. Before Caleb could ask the obvious question, Mark just scowled further.

"It's not *that*," he said. "But I don't have time for a woman. They need attention. Gifts. Things like that. I have to run my ranch."

"Yes, generally speaking, women do like it when you acknowledge their existence," Caleb said wryly.

Mark only huffed out an annoyed breath.

"I'm only suggesting asking her out, not marrying her. You need to get out of your shell." Harrison finished the last of his coffee. "Believe me, a good woman would do a world of good for you."

"I don't have any interest in dating, and I most especially don't want to date a mousy nurse like her."

Caleb heard the small intake of breath, and to his horror, Abby herself had been within hearing distance of that last statement. She turned white when she realized they'd seen her. To her credit, she didn't burst into tears or throw a plate at Mark's face—all deservedly so. She shrugged, a tight smile on her face.

"Isn't it convenient then that I have no interest in dating asshole ranchers like yourself?" she said lightly.

Mark moved to stand, but it was Harrison who stood first. "Abby, whatever you heard—"

"I heard enough. Have a nice day."

Caleb could almost convince himself she hadn't been affected by Mark's words, but the tension in her shoulders as she left The Rise and Shine spoke otherwise.

"Shit," Mark muttered. "Shit, shit, shit."

"Yeah, shit." Harrison slapped Mark on the back of his head. "You dumbass. Go apologize to her."

"I might wait until she's less likely to murder you," Caleb said. At his brothers' looks, he shrugged. "Believe me, I've been there."

When Megan returned from her kitchen to see one Thornton with his head in his hands, one with an amused smirk on his face, and another with a look of sheer exasperation, she was wise enough not to say a word.

CHAPTER TEN

"I hope you like sushi," Caleb said after he and Megan were seated at a booth in the corner, "because otherwise tonight won't be much fun for you."

Megan wrinkled her nose. "Lucky for you that I do like sushi. Although what would've happened if I'd said I hated it? Would you go somewhere else with me?"

He heaved a deep sigh. "I guess. Although I would've judged you for it for the entire evening."

Laughing, Megan felt her nerves calm for the first time that evening. Ever since Caleb had come into The Rise and Shine and insisted that she go to dinner with him, she'd been a mess. Actually, she'd been a mess over him for what felt like an eternity. Now that she was sitting across from him, his dark hair tousled and his face showing the shadow of his beard already, she had to stop herself from practically crawling into his lap and eating him up. It didn't help that he was wearing a button-up that brought out the green in his eyes, or that he looked at her like he could eat her up, too, if given half the chance.

Megan drank almost her entire glass of water before they'd even ordered.

"What are you getting?" Caleb asked as he set down his menu.

"The sashimi platter. And no, I'm not sharing, although I do appreciate that you'll be paying for it."

He tipped his head back and laughed, and she drank in the lines of his throat as he laughed. *He's way too handsome,* she thought petulantly. If only he had a receding hairline, or a paunch, or overly long nose hair. Something to temper his handsomeness and make him less intimidating in that regard. It didn't help that their waitress eyed him with obvious interest, or that other women in the restaurant had almost fallen out of their chairs when he'd walked in.

Megan scowled. She didn't have time to deal with a man as handsome as Caleb Thornton. Didn't she know going out with him would be bad news?

When Caleb gave her a glance that sent her body aflame, she cleared her throat and asked, "Any news about my favorite criminal?"

Caleb frowned. "Nothing yet. It's like this guy is a fucking ghost. We did have a tip today that I hope will give us something more substantial to investigate."

Megan's ears perked up. "Really?"

"I shouldn't tell you this, but I'm not on duty right now. This same guy was spotted at Clover Park yesterday evening. A woman was jogging and noticed he was following her."

"Is she all right?"

He nodded. "She arrived home before he could do anything, but he also didn't wear a mask over his face this time. She was able to identify that he has a scar on his lower lip about three inches long. That's not exactly something you see on a lot of people, so it helps us for obvious reasons."

Megan sat back in her booth, considering. Once they caught this guy, Caleb wouldn't be around her bakery anymore, would he? Their association would end, and she couldn't stop her throat from closing at the thought. It was stupid, but she didn't want it to end. Caleb drove her crazy. She wanted to strangle him almost as often as she wanted to kiss him. And yet…through all of this, he'd been her one constant.

She smiled wanly. "I'm glad you got something legitimate. I'm tired of looking over my shoulder, afraid that he's found me and is going to do whatever it is he thinks he wants to do."

"I won't let that happen," he vowed. "He won't put a finger on you—not on my watch."

"I know."

Their entrees soon arrived, and the evening was taken up with eating and enjoying each other. Megan playfully slapped his hand away when he tried to snag some of her sashimi, while she stole multiple pieces of tempura when he wasn't looking. He told her he'd get his revenge for that, which only made her shiver with delight.

She also noticed that Caleb didn't order any alcohol. She wondered if her admission that she didn't drink anymore had affected him somehow, or at the very least, he didn't drink out of consideration for her. Her heart swelled.

When she sipped her water, the bite of wasabi hot on her tongue, he pointed his chin at her choice of beverage.

"So you don't drink at all?"

She stilled. Her fingers curling about the cold glass, she struggled to answer. Why was he asking this now? She didn't want to talk about the past. She never wanted to talk about the past because some things were better off left dead and buried, the bones disintegrating into the earth.

"No, I don't. I haven't since that night." She looked away, refusing to see the pity on his face. His own regrets about that night, when she'd thrown herself at him and he'd pushed her away. Her gut churned and her face heated with embarrassment, even after so many years.

"You were just a dumb kid, you know. Anyone could've gotten screwed up like that. If I had a dollar for how many dumb kids I've arrested for things like that—"

"Don't, Caleb. Please don't." She pushed her food away, no longer hungry. "I really don't want to talk about this."

"Because we've never talked about it. I know you were angry with me for a long time. Are you still angry?"

Her honest answer? She didn't know. Her anger was jumbled up with so many other emotions regarding Caleb that it was difficult to figure out where one thread started and another ended. She'd hated Caleb for many years—for arresting her, for rejecting her. For humiliating her. For indirectly causing her to lose her scholarship and forcing her to stay in Fair Haven when she'd gotten so close to leaving.

"I don't know," she said finally. "It's all so messed up. I wanted to hate you for all eternity. It was easier than confronting what I'd done to screw up my own life."

His eyes darkened, and a well of sadness she'd only glimpsed before shimmered in his eyes. "I get it. I do. You're not the only one who's fucked up." He pushed his fingers through his hair. "Honestly, if anyone were to win that battle, it would be me."

She frowned in confusion. As far as she knew, Caleb

Thornton had been a model citizen since he'd been born. He'd gotten good grades, had played sports, had graduated with honors and attended college before returning home to become a police officer. He'd worked his way up in the ranks with determination and sheer hard work.

The look on his face prompted her to say more than she would have otherwise. Perhaps it was the hint of vulnerability in his expression, or her desire to discover what he'd done that still haunted him. Maybe if she opened up, he would as well.

"I think I hated you the most when you told me I was a child when I tried to kiss you." His eyes widened at that, but she just shook her head. "I wanted to seem like an adult, but you destroyed that. You reminded me that I didn't know a damn thing—especially when it came to men."

"Megan, you know good and well that even if I'd wanted you then, I couldn't have acted on it. You were all of seventeen."

"I was going to be eighteen in a month, and you aren't that much older than me. Don't act like you wanted me then. I know your feelings have changed—I think they have—but back then—"

He gritted his teeth. "Do you really think that I don't want you *now?*"

"Considering the hot-and-cold act you like to play, yes." His tone sparked anger deep inside her, and she rather wished they would start fighting again. She could understand fighting with Caleb Thornton. It was the softer moments—the vulnerable moments—where she lost her footing.

"Considering how I kissed you that night in your apartment, and at your bakery today, I think it's fairly clear that I want you."

"Because I'm a challenge. Because I pushed you away the last time we kissed, and you wanted to prove to yourself that you can conquer me. I can just be another notch on your bedpost."

She didn't know where these words were coming from, yet they fell from her mouth like a torrent. Perhaps they'd been buried deep inside her all along, just waiting to be freed. Her doubts clawed at her soul, drawing blood. *Why would he want me now when he'd never really wanted me before?*

And perhaps the greatest question of all: *Who would really want me when no one ever had before?*

They stared at each other, at a stalemate. Caleb seemed incredulous, while Megan wanted to shake him until his teeth rattled.

"If you really think that, then you're not as intelligent as I thought you were."

She stood up and grabbed her purse. "Go to hell, Caleb. I don't have time for this and I don't have time for your bullshit, either."

Stalking out of the restaurant, Megan didn't know where she would go. Caleb had picked her up, and it was too far to walk home. And she wasn't particularly in the mood to walk home at night when the last time she'd done just that, she'd been followed and almost accosted by some creep.

She rubbed her arms as shivers wracked her frame. It wasn't cold outside, but she felt cold. Numb. She gritted her teeth to keep them from chattering.

"Megan! Megan, dammit, wait!" Caleb grabbed her by the elbow. She pulled away. "What the hell was that all about?" he demanded.

"Just leave me alone. Please. I want to go home. I can't

keep doing this with you. All we ever do is fight." She sounded pathetic, desperate, and she was completely exhausted. And above all else, she hated herself for starting this fight in the first place, because it was easier to fight with Caleb than love him.

Her chills only increased with that admission. *I can't love him,* she thought, but she knew it was pointless.

She'd fallen in love with him ages ago before she'd even realized it. Now she was too far in to stop it.

Caleb put his hands on her shoulders as he turned her to face him. "What are we doing, Megan? What is this? Is this really about how I don't want you?"

He wrapped her in his arms, and she could only surrender. His body was hard, and he practically shook with anger. Or maybe it was sheer lust. Megan couldn't know anymore.

"You're an idiot if you think I feel anything for you but complete obsession. You've driven me crazy ever since you tried to kiss me that night when I arrested you. I've wanted you for years, but I told myself you needed a better man than me."

He seemed to struggle for words. "But now? I don't care. I don't care about all of the times I said I'd stay away from you." He gripped her so tightly she could barely breathe. "You're mine, Megan Flannigan, and I don't give a flying fuck if that pisses you off."

He kissed her ruthlessly, and she could only hang onto him. Digging her nails into his shoulders, she opened her mouth to him. He stroked inside her mouth like she knew he would stroke inside her body. She didn't care that they were standing in the middle of the restaurant's parking lot, or that anyone could see them under the streetlamp.

She didn't care about anything but being held in Caleb's arms.

"I'm taking you home now. If you don't want to, you better say it now."

She buried her face in his neck. "Take me home with you," she whispered. She tilted her head back so she could look him in the eye. "Take me home and make me yours."

His breaths came in pants, his heart hammering against his sternum. She kissed him there, right above his pounding heart, and he groaned. It was a groan of surrender, and she knew he'd finally given himself up to this as much as she had.

She barely remembered the ride back to his place. When they arrived, he opened her car door and hauled her into his arms, carrying her into his house. She took in the masculine furniture, the darkly painted walls, and even the artwork framed on the walls, but it all faded away when Caleb set her down and kissed her. He cupped her face in his hands, gentleness replacing the desperation of earlier.

"You sure about this?" he asked. "I don't want you to do something you'll regret."

"I could never regret this. I've wanted this as long as you have." She brushed his dark hair from his forehead in a tender caress. "I'm sorry for what I said. It was stupid of me. I ruined our date because I'm an *idiot*—"

"Don't. It doesn't matter. Nothing matters except that you're here with me."

Her heart clamored in her chest as she backed away. He raised an eyebrow, but he didn't move to stop her. With unsteady movements, she began to unbutton her blouse. Even though her fingers trembled, she watched his face the entire time. She stripped out of her blouse and tossed it to the floor;

it fluttered down like a pink bird until it landed in a haphazard heap.

He licked his lips and made a move to approach her, but she shook her head. Steadier now, she unzipped her jeans and pushed them down to her ankles, kicking off her flats in the process. Now clad only in her black lace bra and panties, she let him drink her in. Appreciation showed clearly on his face, and based on how hard he was clenching his fists at his sides, he was barely leashing his hunger.

She let her hair tumble down her shoulders before she reached behind her back to unhook her bra. Her breasts were heavy and her nipples ached, and the brush of the lace against her nipples made her shiver. As Caleb watched, she tossed her bra to the floor. She cupped her breasts as she approached him.

She took his hands in hers and lifted them to cup her breasts, replacing her touch with his. His jaw clenched, but he didn't move. She smiled a smile as old as Eve.

She kissed that tight jaw, that delicious line that led to his shoulder. She inhaled his scent, and the smell went straight to her aching core. Taking his right hand, she placed it under the waistband of her panties, his palm pressing against her sex.

He swore. He couldn't stop himself from petting her nipple with one hand and her sex with the other. Closing her eyes, Megan breathed deeply.

She could almost feel when Caleb's control snapped. Growling, he pulled her into his arms and raced up the stairs to his bedroom.

Linking her arms around his neck, she could only laugh softly in sheer delight.

CHAPTER ELEVEN

Caleb couldn't help but feel like this moment was sacred, like he'd been waiting his whole life for it. As he gazed down at Megan's upturned face, he wanted to pour out his heart to her. Expose the inside of his soul, black and blue as it was, and beg her for absolution.

Of course, it wasn't that simple, and he didn't deserve something like that. While she'd been honest and apologetic, he hadn't said a word about his own secrets. A voice whispered in his ear—*fraud, coward*—but he pushed it aside.

This wasn't the time. He'd tell her at some point. Just not right now, when he had more important things to worry about.

He laid her on the bed, almost reverently. He flipped on a lamp, and she looked like she had been dipped in sunshine. She almost glowed, like some kind of fairy creature. But when she sat up, a mischievous smile on her face, she was all human —and all Megan.

She crooked a finger at him. "Come to bed, Officer," she purred.

His cock hardened to the point that it was painful, and he struggled to take off his clothes fast enough. It didn't help that Megan lay back on *his* bed, her breasts up-thrust, wearing nothing but that scrap of lace she called panties.

When his belt refused to be unbuckled, he decided he'd just pounce on her. He'd take care of logistics later. She giggled when he encased her between his arms and legs, and before he could kiss her, she was pulling his head down for her kiss.

She tasted like strawberries, and rainbows, and lightning storms, and God Almighty, he was turning into a poet, and a bad one at that. If he weren't careful, he'd kneel at her feet and pen an ode to her purple-painted toenails. *God, I'm in deep.* The thought should've terrified him, but it only confirmed his own swirling emotions.

He was obsessed with the scattering of moles behind her right ear; the circuitous pattern of freckles around her collarbone; the way her hair shimmered with the colors of a sunset. But he also loved that her belly was slightly rounded, that she had a scar in the shape of a crescent moon on her upper left forearm, and that she made a face—a face that was a cross between consternation and absolute want—when he touched her. Her eyebrows furrowed, and her eyes narrowed, and it amused him more than he'd expected.

He almost wanted to tell her, but he decided that although he'd done many stupid things in his life, telling a woman she looked amusing when she was lying naked underneath him would be the height of idiocy.

Kissing his way down her neck, he pushed her breasts up as he licked the soft skin underneath them. She mewled, a desperate sound, and he reveled in it. He thumbed her nipples before he lightly pinched them, and they became swollen red berries that he longed to suckle. Giving into what he wanted, he pulled one into his mouth, the silkiness of her skin beyond anything he could've imagined. She ran her fingers through his hair, murmuring his name, as he sucked one nipple and then the other.

The night at her apartment filled his memory, and he could taste her on his tongue already. But he wanted to see more of her, and with a quick movement, he moved so she lay on her stomach. He palmed her ass, barely concealed by her lace panties.

Megan looked at him over her shoulder. "Should I ask what you're doing?" she said, her voice husky.

Caleb traced patterns on her ass before spanking it with a light slap. She yelped, which only made him slap the other cheek. That second smack earned him an appreciative purr, and Megan stretched onto his bed like a cat in heat.

Dipping his fingers into the waistband of her panties, he pulled them down her waist and off of her until she was completely naked. His mouth watered at all of that creamy nudity splayed on his bed, her ass slightly red from his spanking. He was still fully clothed, and the contrast of their two states of dress only heightened the sexual tension.

Megan looked like she wanted to flip over again, but he held her down. With gentle hands, he parted her legs, revealing first the patch of auburn curls on her mound, and then the pink petals of her sex. They already gleamed with moisture, and when he slicked a finger through them, she shivered.

He kissed the small of her back, his fingers petting her, feeling her hips rise with each of his touches. Swirling her wetness through her folds, he nipped the arch of one buttock and then the other. Megan's breathing increased, and a flush began to cover her back to her shoulders. He licked at the salty sweat beading on her back as he pushed a finger inside her, the heel of his hand pressing against her clit.

"Oh just like that, harder," she moaned. "I need you so badly, Caleb."

He stroked her with his finger, at first slowly, and then faster, his hand brushing her clit with each thrust. Her body tightened, and when he added another finger, she squealed. Wetness coated his entire hand, and the sounds of his pounding into her only made his own body practically vibrate with need. His cock strained against his jeans.

Megan bucked and writhed. He drank in the sight of her losing control, and it was the most beautiful thing he'd ever seen. When he pumped his finger one last time, she came, her head tilted back and her body shaking. Her sheath contracted around his fingers in a vice-like grip. Gently rubbing her clit a little longer, he withdrew, standing over her to undress.

She turned over, her body flushed and perspiring, her hair tangled about her shoulders. She watched with a lazy gaze as he stripped out of his clothes, but Megan wasn't some passive partner. When his cock was unveiled, she sat up and reached for him with a sensual smile. With her face so close to his cock and her hands busy around his shaft, he had to grit his teeth until he was sure they were going to turn into nubs.

That tongue of hers licked him from root to tip; his toes curled into the carpet. A vein alongside the length of his cock pulsed in time with his heartbeat.

"I had a feeling you'd be packing, but this is definitely a surprise." She smiled even wider as she swirled her tongue around the sensitive crown. "I'm not sure you're going to fit, though. I've never had a guy as big as you."

He grimaced, but only because he was afraid he wouldn't be able to go slow enough for her. Closing his eyes, he tried to think of ice baths and cold showers, but it didn't help. When she cupped his balls with her palm, he cursed and pushed her without ceremony back onto the bed.

Before he climbed on top of her, he fished in his bedside drawer for a condom. After ripping open the foil packet after a few tries, Megan biting her lip to restrain a giggle, he fell upon her. Kissing her with open-mouthed desperation, their tongues tangled as Megan bent her knees right as his cock brushed her wet curls.

"I don't know if I can go slow," he admitted. "I've wanted you for too long. But if I hurt you, just tell me, and I'll stop—"

She placed a finger against his lip. "You won't hurt me. I want you. I want you inside me." She kissed him before whispering, "Make love to me, Caleb."

Megan didn't realize she was holding her breath, but when Caleb began to press inside her, she had to gasp for air. Not out of discomfort, but because she hadn't known what it would truly feel like to have him within her like this. She'd imagined it so many times, but to have his length fill her, his arms and legs enclosing her, and his gaze glued to her own—it was more than she could've ever imagined.

She swallowed, her throat dry. Her heart pounded until she could feel it in her temples. Finally, he was completely inside her, and they both let out moans at the same time.

Megan brushed Caleb's hair from his forehead, where it was damp with perspiration, and he closed his eyes at her touch. His arms trembled.

When he didn't move, she hitched her hips upward. He opened his eyes, his pupils blown wide. Finally, he started to move.

Megan shook; she begged. She scratched his chest, his shoulders, his upper arms. He pulled out of her only to slam back in, and her eyes rolled back in her head. Clutching at the sheets, she couldn't help but wonder if she would simply drift away from so much pleasure. Intense, enveloping pleasure, the kind that she'd never thought was possible.

Caleb took her and claimed her. She knew after this, she'd never get him out of her heart—even if she wanted to. She kissed his chest and pulled his head down to kiss her as he pounded into her. Hooking her legs over his arms, he opened her so wide that she didn't know how she would be able to stand it. She almost pleaded for him to stop because she was going to shatter. Not simply from desire, but from the inside out.

"Fuck, baby, God," he growled in her ear. They kissed again, a meeting of lips and teeth and moans, and he sped his movements. With each movement, he brushed her clit, and Megan felt herself growing wetter and tighter. The bed squeaked under them.

She started coming within moments, her belly tightening, and she gasped and screamed as she coiled higher and higher. Caleb only pumped into her harder, and with one last thrust, she burst into a million bits of light. Her throat hurt, and she only realized later it was from gasping and panting and screaming his name. She came and came, and she vaguely heard Caleb shout her name as he came, too.

They collapsed into a sweaty heap, Caleb on top of her. She knew in a few minutes she'd ask him to move because he was heavy, but at the moment, she loved feeling his weight on top of her. Their bodies were sweat-slicked and smelling of sex and salt. Licking the side of his neck, she smiled when he grunted.

With a kiss, Caleb rose from the bed, murmuring something that Megan couldn't really hear. She yawned. She hadn't been this tired—like a rag doll that had been completely wrung out—in ages. She smiled dreamily as she closed her eyes. She heard water running and then Caleb climbed back into bed with her and pulled her into his arms.

If she heard the words she'd dreamt of hearing in those moments between consciousness, she told herself in the morning she'd only been dreaming.

It was still dark when Megan opened her eyes to the feeling of hands on her body. She smiled as those hands cupped her breasts—her nipples still sensitive from earlier ministrations—and she flipped over to face Caleb when his hand trailed down her belly.

"What time is it?" she asked in a whisper.

"I don't know. Early."

She could barely make out his face in the dim light. Before he'd come back to bed, he'd switched off the lamp, plunging his bedroom into almost total darkness, thanks to the blackout curtains hanging from his windows. A little bit of light shone through the edges, but Megan rather felt like they were both formless figures floating somewhere.

She touched his face with gentle fingers. Stubble rubbed against her fingertips, and she laughed softly when he kissed her fingers. He had an indentation on his left cheek—a small scar?—and she discovered a tiny mole near his right ear. His hair was silky soft, and she ran her fingers through it for a few moments. Caleb arched into her touch like a cat wanting to be petted.

Really, if she thought about it, Caleb and Gary were rather alike: they wanted to be stroked, fed, and then they wanted to cuddle with you. Then again, she thought with an inner laugh, Gary certainly couldn't kiss her like Caleb was doing right now.

This time, their lovemaking was languid. They touched each other without the feeling that it was the last time it would happen. Megan enjoyed discovering the textures of Caleb's body—hard muscle, springy hair, soft patches hidden by his clothes during the day—while Caleb did the same. He stroked her belly, the inside of her elbow, the sides of her torso. When he tickled the indentation of her waist, she squealed, trying to curve into a protective ball.

"No, not there, Caleb!" She giggled like mad as he tickled her. Gasping for breath, she finally pushed him away and climbed on top of him, pinning him down to the bed.

"Be a good boy and stay there," she commanded. She felt his cock harden under her, and she smiled in the darkness. Holding his wrists to the bed, she shimmied against him, rubbing her wetness against his lengthening cock. Groaning, he tried to break free from her grip, but she held firm. Then again, she had a feeling he could tip her over and have his way with her in seconds. She appreciated that he let her play—at least for the time being.

With the darkness came the insatiable need to fill it with words. Megan had never been much for dirty talk in bed. Usually it was embarrassing, if not downright crass, and anytime a boyfriend had tried it she'd erupted into laughter and the mood had been killed. Now, though, she didn't feel that way. She felt triumphant—and infinitely sexy.

Pushing her fingers through her folds while letting go of one of Caleb's wrists, she gasped to find the moisture already pooled there. In a breathless voice, she murmured, "You make me so wet, Caleb. You don't even have to touch me. I think of you and I get wet."

He inhaled a tight breath. His hips bucked under her with a slight movement. "How wet are you, baby? Tell me."

"So wet that my hand is almost soaked." She took his hand and pressed it to her sex. "Feel it for yourself."

His long fingers parted her, and he cursed, long and low and desperate. Vibrating with need, he seemed to be barely restrained from taking her right then and there.

He played with her, stroking her and laving her with her own wetness, and she pushed against his hand with every touch. Her body curled in on itself, and she knew an orgasm was close. So close.

But Caleb wasn't going to let that happen so easily. He slid down the bed until her sex was right above his mouth. Megan panted when she felt his hot breath against her center. Her legs quivered in anticipation. When he slid his tongue through her petals, she had to bite her lip to keep from screaming in sheer pleasure. He held her there, even when she wanted to buck and shake. He was ruthless. He lapped at her, like he couldn't get enough of her taste, and she gripped the head-board to keep herself from collapsing.

He tongued her before sucking on one of her folds and then the other. Megan had never been taken like this, with such ruthless tenderness. She tipped her head back, her back in a graceful arch, as Caleb thrust his tongue inside her hot sheath.

"Fuck, you taste good. I can't get enough of you." He finally began to circle her clit, but so lightly that it wasn't nearly enough.

She wanted to beg him to suck her clit so hard that she came, but at the same time, she never wanted this to end. Her body tightened to such an extent that it was almost painful.

"Please, Caleb," she heard herself beg. "Please, please."

His fingers dug into her hips to hold her steady. He licked her—long and thoroughly—one last time before he suckled her clit. The pressure shot a bolt of ecstasy through Megan, and soon she reached her peak. She dug her fingers into the headboard as she came, and the only reason she didn't fall down was Caleb holding her up.

She hadn't even finished coming when Caleb tossed her onto the bed, fumbled for a condom in the bedside drawer, and filled her in one heavy thrust. Her orgasm continued with his penetration, and he pounded into her. Wrapping her arms and legs around him, she could feel another orgasm coiling deep within her belly. Her eyes rolled back into her head when she felt Caleb's cock twitch inside her as his orgasm burst upon him, and he filled her over and over again as she shuddered and shook for a second time.

She couldn't move. She could barely breathe. She gasped, and he gasped, and she couldn't untangle her legs from his.

They had become like one entity, and Megan's heart was close to bursting.

Kissing her gently behind her ear, on her cheek, on her forehead, Caleb said her name in a quiet voice that only further proved what she already knew.

She was in love with Caleb Thornton.

CHAPTER TWELVE

When Caleb dropped her off at her house later that morning, he said once again, "I'll just be at the station. Call me if you need anything, okay?"

Megan was torn between complete happiness that she and Caleb were together and worry about what people would say when they would find out. Would people think Caleb was slumming it, like Harrison had done with Sara, according to more narrow-minded people? Megan shuddered inwardly.

She'd almost told Caleb that she would drive herself home this morning, but he'd insisted. She couldn't stop herself from glancing out the window at the street outside, wondering if anyone was watching them.

Caleb sensed her unease, but not for the correct reasons. "Do you want me to stay with you? I can call off work, or I can tell Gonzalez that this took precedence today—"

"No, no, I'll be fine." She smiled. Although she had a feeling Caleb didn't really believe her. "Really. You need to get to work, and so do I." Feeling guilty, she kissed him. Then she almost regretted kissing him, because she didn't want that kiss to end.

They were both breathing hard when they pulled apart. "That definitely didn't help my self-control," Caleb muttered.

Megan laughed as she got out of the car. "See you later, Officer. Have a good day." She saluted him.

He tipped his police cap to her before driving away. Megan watched him drive off, sighing as he turned the corner and disappeared. Going inside, she collapsed on the couch and tried to make heads and tails of what had happened last night.

"I slept with Caleb Thornton," she said aloud. "Twice." Gary hopped into her lap, giving her a judgmental lock only cats could manage. She stroked his head as she said the words again: "I slept with Caleb. And it was amazing."

She petted Gary absently, her mind whirling. Or maybe it was just that her body wouldn't stop tingling. It didn't help that she'd realized she was in love with Caleb, and if she were truly honest with herself, she would also admit she'd been in love with him for a long time.

Perhaps it hadn't been love at first—not when he'd arrested her, certainly. There'd been attraction, of course. She'd looked at him from afar for a number of years until he'd left Fair Haven, and she'd put him out of her mind as best as she could. Then he'd returned, a newly minted police officer, and Megan's teenage crush had only blossomed.

But when she'd been seventeen and reckless, it hadn't been love. It had been more akin to hate after he'd rejected her and pushed her aside. So how had hate transformed into love? Or maybe it hadn't been hate at all, but a longing for another person to recognize your existence?

She didn't know. She was too exhausted, too happy, too terrified. She wished with all of her heart that everything would work out in their favor, but she knew that life rarely went that simply.

When she heard the knock on her front door, she nearly jumped out of her skin. Gary woke up, all claws, and she yelped when he dug said claws right into her breast. She pushed him off of her chest and glared at him while he glared back.

"Damn cat," she muttered as she went to get the door. Who would be looking for her now? Caleb? Had he decided not to go to the station after all?

Megan blinked when she opened the door. Ruth stood there, her red hair gleaming in the sunlight. She looked concerned.

"Megan, there you are. Why haven't you answered your phone? We've been worried about you." Ruth moved to step inside, and although Megan rather wished she could tell her mother to go away, she didn't have the energy.

Megan pulled her phone from her purse, seeing all of the missed texts and phone calls once she plugged it in to charge it. She winced. Missed calls from Sara, her mom, Jubilee. She blushed when she realized that many of the calls had been when she'd been with Caleb. In his bed. Having more orgasms than she could count.

"Sorry. I didn't know the battery had died." Megan sat down next to Ruth, hoping that this was a quick visit. "I only just got in this morning."

Ruth gave her a look that said she knew what that last statement meant, but she didn't comment on it. Instead, she said, "Why didn't you tell me about the man who followed you home? I had to find out from one of those busybodies in town instead of my own daughter." Hurt filled Ruth's face. "Are you all right? Have they caught this man yet?"

Megan wanted to rub her temples, a headache already forming. "I'm sorry I didn't tell you. I got so caught up with everything that I wasn't thinking."

"You found the time to tell Sara."

Megan winced. She had texted Sara the morning after, mostly so Sara wouldn't have to hear it from somebody else. She'd mistakenly assumed Sara would've told their mother, as Sara—along with James—lived with Ruth at the moment. Megan hadn't thought Sara would keep that a secret. Then again, Sara had probably sensed that Megan didn't want the story spreading any more than it would have. And if she were really honest, she'd admit that Sara had probably assumed— or hoped—that Megan would tell Ruth herself.

"Look, I had a late night. I need to get ready for work. Can we talk about this later?" Megan rose, hoping Ruth would get the hint that she wanted her to leave.

Ruth, though, didn't get up, her expression still full of hurt. If Megan didn't know better, she saw tears shimmering in her mother's eyes.

All of the old emotions—resentment, disgust, fear, anger —filled Megan like a tidal wave, and the headache pushing at her skull began to intensify. She couldn't reconcile the woman sitting here with the woman Ruth had once been. Or more accurately, Megan couldn't suddenly act like a daughter to a mother who hadn't mothered her children when they'd most needed it.

"Were you with Caleb Thornton?" Ruth asked suddenly.

Megan stilled. She'd never talked about Caleb with her

mother, mostly because she'd never felt like it was any of Ruth's business. Ruth knew that Caleb had arrested Megan all those years ago, and she probably had some inkling of the combative attraction between them. She'd never asked Megan before, though.

Megan sat back down, albeit reluctantly. "If I say yes, will you let me get ready for work already?"

"Megan, be careful. The Thorntons..." Ruth shook her head. "That mother of theirs put your sister through hell. Do you really think she'll change her mind about you? She'll try to tear you and Caleb apart the second she gets wind of what's happening."

Megan had to disagree, only because she knew Caleb wouldn't let that happen. He'd seen what Lisa Thornton had done when she'd interfered in Harrison and Sara's relationship; he wouldn't allow Lisa to meddle like that a second time.

"It's fine," Megan replied, perhaps more to herself than to Ruth. "And why are you saying this? Are you saying we shouldn't be together?"

Ruth shook her head. "No, not at all. Just that you should be careful, that's all. I don't want another daughter of mine hurt like that. And given your history with this man..." The words died away, but Megan felt them in her gut anyway.

Yes, her history. They had history—that much was true. All of the doubts that had plagued Megan came roaring back, and she had to clench her fists to keep her trembling from showing. *What if this is doomed to fail?* she couldn't help but think. *What if we can't overcome our pasts, no matter how hard we try?*

That anger toward Ruth only intensified, because at the moment, she was Megan's only available target. Ruth didn't have the right to warn Megan, like she had ever been a real parent to her. Where had Ruth been when Megan had needed her after her arrest? When she'd been swimming in a mire of shame and guilt and self-hatred? Ruth hadn't even noticed because she'd been too busy getting drunk.

"I know we have a history, but honestly, I don't see how it's any of your business." Megan tried to sound cool, but she knew she sounded bitter more than anything. "I get where you're coming from, but it's unnecessary. Caleb and I will figure it out on our own. I think we both know that people trying to interfere in other people's relationships never ends well for anyone."

Ruth looked hurt, and Megan couldn't help but notice the deep lines on her mother's face. Ruth was sixty now, and her years of drinking hadn't been kind to her. Although she looked healthier sober, she would never be able to escape the damage done to both her appearance—deep lines, broken capillaries, loose skin—and her internal organs. It was a miracle her liver still worked at all.

Ruth frowned deeply, those lines only intensifying on her face. "Why can't we talk anymore?" she asked in a plaintive voice. "Your sister and I have mended our relationship, but you won't even consider it. Am I going to be the bad guy forever?"

It was on the tip of Megan's tongue to say yes, but she restrained herself. Barely. She couldn't help but remember the days and nights when Ruth hadn't made sure that her daughters had enough to eat, or decent clothes to wear to school, or shoes without holes in them. She hadn't been there when Sara had suffered from terrible rumors during high school; she hadn't been there when Megan had been arrested.

And there was the crux of Megan's anger, because within

its core was sheer terror—terror that she would turn out just like Ruth. It was ironic that Megan's arrest had been because of drinking; or rather, it had been fitting. Megan had her mother's blood flowing through her veins. What if she became just like her? Bitter, angry, fueled by drink and nothing else. Negligent and selfish. Even though Ruth was sober now and could definitively say she was not like the woman she used to be, the old Ruth still haunted her and everyone who'd known her. She was a ghost that could never be fully exorcised.

The terror swirled until it settled in Megan's gut, hard and heavy. *I can't end up like her*, she whispered. *I have to be better than her.*

Her arrest had been a wake-up call, but it had also instilled in her the message that one false move would send her straight into the spiral that Ruth had been stuck in for over twenty years.

Megan swallowed against the lump in her throat. "I'm not like Sara," she said in a hoarse voice. "I'm not going to forgive and forget and act like everything is roses. Do you have any idea what you did to me? To us? Forgive me if I'm not particularly interested in being nice to a woman who doesn't know the first thing about being a real mother."

Ruth flinched. Guilt assailed Megan, but she pushed it away.

"I know you're still angry, and you have every right to be. I can't say sorry enough. It won't bring back those years." Ruth wiped at her eyes. "But I don't want you to stay like this. You can't let anger rule your life. I did, and it only ends up making you miserable."

"Nice words, but I'm not biting. Talk is cheap, and that's

all I've been hearing lately: talk." Megan gestured toward the front door. "I need to get ready for work."

Ruth didn't need another hint. "I'll call you later, then." When she reached the door, she hesitated. Looked over her shoulder.

"What is it?"

Ruth just shook her head. "It doesn't matter, because talk is cheap, right?" She smiled grimly before leaving Megan to herself.

CALEB ARRIVED at the station that morning, his brain trying to concentrate, but it was almost pointless. It was full of Megan: Megan in his bed, in his arms, arching under him. Megan smiling, Megan moaning. When he'd seen a woman with red hair enter the station, his heart had pounded until he'd realized it was someone else.

He almost slapped himself for being so obvious, but it wouldn't have made any difference. Last night had been perfect, amazing, glorious. Mind-blowing. His entire body remembered, and dammit if he didn't get an erection just sitting at his computer.

"You look happy today," Gonzalez said, his tone clearly amused. He sat down in a chair across from Caleb. "Now I'm dying to know why."

Caleb shifted in his chair and tried to wipe the loopy grin from his face. "It's nothing. Have you gotten anything more on our guy?"

"Nice subject change. We did get something. There was a report of a man with a similar scar committing petty thefts down in Seattle, and he was caught on camera at a local 7-11 in the Fremont area recently." Gonzalez motioned for Caleb to open some files that had been added to the station's shared drive. "Here's the video from Seattle PD. I doubt there are too many other guys with scars like that running around in western Washington."

Caleb watched as the man who'd been terrorizing Megan stole a number of candy bars, sodas, and cigarettes before exiting the 7-11. If he didn't know the man was dangerous, he would've laughed at the random robbery for junk food.

"So we have our guy. Do we know how to find him?" Caleb asked.

"We're working on it. He's stopped committing bigger crimes because he knows we're getting close." Gonzalez sat back in his chair and gave Caleb a slow smile. "Now that we're all up to speed, tell me why you came in looking like you won the lottery. It wouldn't have anything to do with the woman at the center of all of this, would it?"

Caleb couldn't help but feel like he was in elementary school again, the teacher asking him if he had, in fact, put that frog on Tiffany Anderson's shoulder on the playground. Except that this time, he hadn't done anything wrong, and two, he was a grown-ass man.

"Since when did you become this fucking nosy?" Caleb tried to sound irritated, but it didn't deter Gonzalez one bit.

"Since I've been your supervisor since you started here, and I've watched you and Megan Flannigan go at it like two Tom cats in an alley. I had a feeling being this close to her would cause something to happen. So, are you dating now or what?"

Caleb didn't know the answer to that. Were they dating?

Or were they just hooking up? He frowned at his computer screen. He really needed to talk to Megan about all of this, but at the same time, that might result in something he didn't want to hear. Like she had only wanted him for a night and that was it.

Now he downright scowled.

"I don't know what we are," he finally admitted. "It's...complicated."

"Isn't it always? Just don't make that your Facebook relationship status, though. Johnny did that with his last girl, and she almost assassinated him." Gonzalez laughed. "At any rate, talk to her. Tell her how you feel. *Really* feel. Women want your heart on a silver platter and nothing else. They know when you're half-assing it. Believe me."

"Is that how you got Gretchen to marry you?" Caleb asked wryly.

"You bet your ass it is. I had to grovel and show her I was the best man for the job. She finally decided I was worth it and it's the best thing that's ever happened to me." He pointed at Caleb. "Don't be a dumbass and let a woman like Megan leave you because you had too much pride to grovel."

Caleb knew Gonzalez was right, and he told himself he would take his advice and be honest with her. About everything. The old fear coalesced in his stomach, and he hated that it could still cause him to break out into a cold sweat. He remembered the lights, the screams, the impact...the sight of Daniel's body as they pulled him from the wreckage. The look on Stephanie Finley's face when she saw Caleb at school months later.

He realized he was breathing hard, and he forced back the panic. Wiping his forehead, he got to work. Another officer would be patrolling near The Rise and Shine today, although Caleb didn't like it when he wasn't near Megan. If he'd already lost one friend. What would happen if he lost someone like Megan?

By the afternoon, he'd been able to focus on the case at hand, but everything crashed to a standstill when he checked his personal email on his phone. When he saw the sender's name, he couldn't believe it.

Stephanie Finley: Daniel's mother.

Why would Stephanie Finley be emailing him now? What in the world did she even have to say to him? Did she want to tell him how much she hated that he hadn't been the one who'd been killed instead? Caleb stared at the email, the innocuous yet vague subject line (*Hello*), and he almost deleted the email without reading it.

But he didn't deserve not to read it.

He opened it, his pulse pounding in his temples. As he began to read, expecting the worst, he realized what he'd thought would be the worst couldn't compare to what Stephanie had written to him.

Dear Caleb,

I'm sure you weren't expecting to get an email like this today. I wrote and rewrote this email so many times that it seems like I started it years ago.

You might not remember me, but I was Daniel's mother. Do you remember coming over to our house when you two were in junior high? You and Daniel would play that X-Box for hours, and the only way I could get you to take a break was to tell you dinner was ready. You would always come over to our house, but Daniel only ever went to your house a few times, mostly for your birthday parties. I know how much you loved coming over to a house that wasn't so...well, I'm sure you know. I don't want to say anything against your parents by any means.

But I'm not writing this to reminisce. I've recently moved back to Fair Haven, and I wanted to ask if you wanted to get coffee or lunch sometime. You were the person closest to Daniel before he died, and you're one of the few links left of him.

I won't lie and say that I wasn't angry with you for a long time, but as the years passed, my anger faded. I wanted to remember Daniel —and your friendship with him—more than I wanted to remember how Daniel had died. I've made my peace with what happened. I hope you have as well.

Let me know if you can meet sometime soon.

All the best,

Stephanie

The words blurred until Caleb couldn't see. His eyes were dry, though, because he'd cried so many tears over Daniel that none were left. He felt like the walls were closing in on him, and he had to get out of the station. What if they found out what he'd done?

God, he was a coward.

He almost ran outside, but when he blinked at the bright sunshine, he had no idea where he wanted to go. Aimless, he walked to a nearby park.

All of the memories of that night came flooding back, but more painfully, happier memories came, too: those afternoons playing video games with Daniel, the pranks they played on Caleb's siblings, the long bike rides through the town. The one time they'd tried switching identities in third grade and had both gotten in huge trouble. Lisa Thornton hadn't thought it was funny at all, but Stephanie had barely restrained a smile at the boys' antics.

Playing in the snow, the few times it had actually snowed in Fair Haven; going fishing in a nearby stream behind Daniel's house; the cookies Stephanie would make, and the peanut butter ones she would make just for Caleb. All of it pushed at Caleb's consciousness until he couldn't breathe. He couldn't think, and he could barely parse any of his emotions beyond one that overwhelmed him: guilt.

So much guilt that he drowned in it.

The old panic returned: fear that people would find out what he'd done. Fear that he should've fought his parents about concealing the reality behind Daniel's death. Fear that he could never truly atone for his sins.

How did you find forgiveness when you knew you didn't deserve it and never would?

I need to see Megan, he thought desperately. He should leave her be, because he was a fraud and a coward, but he didn't care. Only in her arms could he find peace and, maybe, absolution.

CHAPTER THIRTEEN

Megan tried not to notice how quiet Caleb seemed that night. She chalked it up to a long day at work, although when she'd tried to ask him about it, he'd brushed her off and then kissed her until she'd almost forgotten what she'd wanted to ask him.

What is he hiding? She didn't want to think that he was hiding anything, but it niggled at her brain all evening as she cooked them dinner.

Megan had never been the girlfriend who cooked and cleaned—well, she would if she had to, but she had gotten irritated with any guy who assumed she had to be the one to do those tasks. But tonight, she wanted to cook for Caleb. Probably because he's a terrible cook, she thought wryly, remembering the burnt batch of scrambled eggs he'd made her at his house that morning.

"What are you making?" he asked her as he wrapped his arms around her from behind.

"It's a surprise." She slapped his hand away when he tried to pilfer a piece of cheese. "No stealing anything!"

He laughed softly, the exhalation warm against her neck. When he started kissing her neck and shoulder, she was torn between pushing him away so she could get dinner ready and taking him by the hand into her bedroom.

To both her consternation and gratitude, Gary chose that moment to hop onto the counter and almost stepped on her cutting board with recently chopped vegetables.

"Gary! Get off of there!" She picked up the cat—who yowled in protest—and placed him on the kitchen floor. Normally she wouldn't care if Gary hung out on her counter as she cooked (she was enough of a crazy cat lady that nothing much bothered her in regards to Gary) but she didn't want Caleb to think she was like that.

He only laughed again, mostly at Gary's annoyed face. Then again, his smashed face had a tendency to give him a look of perpetual disgruntlement.

"He only wants to help." Caleb reached down and picked up Gary, holding him against his chest. Gary started purring like a motor boat the moment Caleb started scratching his ears.

Megan rolled her eyes. "That cat is a traitor." She pointed a finger at Gary. "Who feeds you? Scoops your stinky litter box? Not this guy. Stop acting like he's your favorite."

Gary only closed his eyes and purred louder.

When they sat down to eat dinner in the living room, they both ate in silence for some moments. It wasn't uncomfortable, though, and it felt rather like a pleasant silence between a couple who had known each other for many years. Megan's heart secretly thrilled. She wanted to call Ruth and tell her she had nothing to worry about. Who did she think she was, anyway, warning Megan like that?

"My mom came over after you dropped me off," she said into the silence after she'd finished her piece of quiche.

Caleb's brows rose. Megan hadn't exactly divulged everything about her childhood to him, but he knew enough. "How was that? And what did she want?"

"She thought she needed to warn me." At his confused look, she added, "From you. Your family."

A light red washed over his cheeks. Clearly embarrassed, he just shook his head. "Don't worry about my mom. She's not going to try anything a second time. She's learned her lesson—believe me."

"That's what I told her, but she still had the audacity to warn me, like she was some kind of mother." The old hurt resurfaced. "She wasn't a mother to me or Sara for most of our lives, and now she comes in and acts like that never happened?" She scoffed. "Yeah, right. I'm not really interested in her supposed advice."

Caleb didn't say anything, but he looked concerned. Rubbing her fingers, he said quietly, "Do you want to talk about it?"

She didn't. She never did. She didn't talk about it with Sara, certainly, and not with Ruth. But Caleb's quiet look of reassurance gave her the courage to speak for the first time in what felt like an eternity.

"My mom...well, you know the stories. She was a drunk from the time I was in kindergarten until just a few years ago. She went to rehab so many times I lost count. When I was little, anytime she'd go away to get help, I always hoped that that time, it would stick. She'd come back, no more bottles of vodka in her trunk, and she'd be the mom I wanted her to be. The mom who took us to Girl Scout meetings and baked for bake sales. You know, the normal kind of moms."

"But that didn't happen."

"No, it didn't. She'd always go back to the bottle. When I got older, I knew that anything she said was a lie." Megan chewed the inside of her cheek. "I stopped hoping she'd get better. Mostly I just wanted to get away from her and from this damn town. I hated this place for a long time."

"I'm sorry," Caleb said. He didn't say anything else, but oddly enough, she didn't want him to. She'd heard so many platitudes from people that a simple "I'm sorry" said worlds more.

"Anyway, I was close to getting out of here when, well, you know what happened." She shrugged, still feeling awkward about her arrest. "I got drunk that night, you arrested me, and that was that. I'll be honest, I hated you for a long time." His eyes widened a little at that admission, but he didn't pull away. "I blamed you, even though that was stupid, because it's not like you made me get drunk underage. But I lost my scholarship and I couldn't get out of this town as a result, so you were the easiest target."

She looked into his eyes, her heart in her throat. "I'm sorry for that. It wasn't fair to you. You were just doing your job that night, and I made it harder. I should never have thrown myself at you, either."

His eyes were dark, searching, and Megan had the oddest sensation that he was examining her very soul at that moment. She hated the vulnerability of the moment, but she refused to retreat. She always retreated, didn't she? It was easier than being honest with herself. It was easier to misinterpret your own emotions than confront your own weaknesses.

"I don't blame you." His voice was husky. "I mean, I'll admit that that night I wasn't too fond of you. You put me in an awkward position, but you were young. We've all done stupid shit as kids." She saw him visibly swallow, and his mouth tightened. "You're not alone in that."

Megan studied him: he'd said words like that to her before. What was plaguing Caleb to this extent?

She had a feeling Caleb wasn't going to disclose so easily, though. In an attempt to draw him out, she thought that continuing to be honest about herself might somehow help him, if at least in a roundabout way.

"You know what my greatest fear was?" She looked ahead, and when Gary hopped onto her lap, she petted him with absent strokes. "I was so afraid of turning into my mother, but for whatever reason, I thought that that meant I should drink. Because I was going to prove I could drink but not be like her." She almost laughed at the words because they sounded so...childish."Obviously that wasn't the case. I got drunk and arrested at seventeen. Nice, right? Ever since, though, I haven't drunk anything because I think I'm still afraid of becoming like my mom."

She looked over at Caleb to gauge his reaction. His face was drawn, like he was in pain. She wanted to touch him, but she almost felt like he'd put up a wall around himself.

"You aren't like your mother," he said. "Not even slightly."

"I hope so. It still eats at me, I guess. I also have this irrational hatred for people who drink and hurt others, you know? Including myself. I hate myself for what I did. I'm just glad no one else was hurt."

Caleb looked pained. Megan reached for him, wanting to understand him. She worried that her confession had somehow made him see her differently. Did he think her unbearably petty for hating him for so long? That she hadn't changed from that rebellious teenager? She opened her mouth to ask, her heart thumping painfully, when he laid his forehead against hers.

He rested it there. He breathed her in, his fingers sifting through her hair.

"God, Megan. God. You don't know what you do to me."

She wanted to ask him what he even meant, but he silenced her thoughts with an almost brutal kiss. Leaning her over his arm, he took her mouth like a marauder, and she could only catch a breath before he kissed her again. Thorough kisses, so hot and wet that Megan's body responded instantly.

Caleb laid her down on the couch; Megan only barely noticed Gary jumping onto the back of the couch.

But as they kissed, she sensed that this was only stalling the inevitable. Breaking their embrace, she gazed up at him and took his face in her hands.

"What is it?" She stroked his cheek. "Tell me. Please, Caleb."

His eyes were dark, searching her. He didn't kiss her again, and she ached for him. Finally, he sat up and away from her and pushed his fingers through his hair.

"I should go." He got off the couch and headed to the door.

Megan blinked. She'd expected a lot of things—but not this.

"Don't leave." She took his arm, trying to convince him. "Why can't we talk about whatever it is that's bothering you? Did I say something?"

He gently pushed her away, and that only stoked her frustration. It reminded her of when he'd pushed her away after she'd tried to kiss him, all those years ago. The pity in his eyes only caused the fire in her belly to increase.

"Don't run away from me," she said. "Why is it that I can be honest, but you can't be?"

He inhaled sharply. His face like granite, he stepped away from her before opening the door. "I should go. I'll see you tomorrow at the bakery. Lock your door and all of your windows tonight. We're getting close to catching this guy and he seems to have gone into hiding, but you should be careful regardless."

This was his police officer voice, detached and unemotional. Megan wanted to scream, to shake him until his teeth clattered. Willing her anger to fade so she could speak without saying something she'd regret, she merely nodded tightly.

"Fine. I'll see you later. Maybe then you can tell me what's going on."

She barely saw it—but the flash of pain on his face melted her frustration. Her heart hurting, she embraced him. He was stiff in her arms for a moment until he melted. Hugging her so tightly she could barely breathe, he muttered her name in her ear before he finally walked out the door.

CHAPTER FOURTEEN

Jubilee sighed and leaned against the counter. "I need a break. Or a cup of coffee. Maybe both."

Megan looked at the clock. "You can go on break, but I'll need you back when the afternoon rush hits."

"Aye aye, captain." Jubilee waved hello to the officer stationed outside before beginning her typical walk around the block.

Now it was Megan's turn to sigh. Caleb hadn't been stationed at The Rise and Shine in the last five days, and she'd barely heard from him. When she texted, he was vague, saying he was busy with work. She had seen a cop car outside her house more than once, though, and she knew that Caleb was keeping an eye on her. He just wasn't *with* her.

Her heart sank into her toes. She'd said too much that night, hadn't she? Now Caleb thought the worst of her, and it was her own fault. Except that realization only made her angry. She wiped down the counter with furious strokes. If he really thought the worst of her now, that was his problem, not hers. She didn't want to be with a guy like that anyway.

She told herself that, but it didn't help the anxiety in her gut. She was halfway tempted to go straight to the station and demand Caleb tell her what was going on. Maybe then he'd finally spill whatever it was he was keeping locked up inside.

Jubilee returned before her break was over, two coffees in her hand. Megan gave her a wry look. "You know we have coffee here, right?"

"Sure, but not like this. Anyway, take it. You look like you could use it." Jubilee eyed Megan over the rim of her cup.

The afternoon rush would be starting soon, and Megan rather wished it would start right now. She didn't want to spill her guts to Jubilee—especially not about her exasperating brother. Yet Megan hadn't talked to anyone about him. Sara had come over to talk about Ruth's visit, and although Megan had confirmed that she and Caleb were...well, something, she hadn't wanted to say anything to her older sister.

"Has Caleb always been evasive?" Megan asked quietly. At Jubilee's look, she explained, "I mean, emotionally. Like he puts up a wall around himself?"

"Ah. I know what you mean." Jubilee fiddled with her coffee's sleeve. "Caleb is one of those people you think you know really well, but then you discover things about him you never even knew were there."

"Meaning...?"

"He's evasive."

Megan sighed. "Do you know why? Or is that just his personality?"

"What's he done? Is he avoiding you?"

A blush crawled up Megan's face, and she busied herself with finishing wiping the counters. "He won't talk to me," she muttered. "I think I freaked him out the other night."

"I think that Caleb is good at reading other people, but not good at reading himself. At least, that's what I've managed to figure out about him as I've gotten older." Jubilee sipped her coffee. "That being said, I'm his little sister, and he left home when I was pretty young. To me, he's the older brother I've always looked up to. He's not as bad as Mark, though. Or Seth. Those two are so mysterious it's a wonder I even know their names." She rolled her eyes.

"I just, I guess I'm worried he hates me now." Megan winced at the pathetic confession, but it was true. It was also deeply ironic, given that she had hated him for so many years. "He's definitely not telling me something, and as of right now, I'm not feeling generous enough not to find out what it is from you."

Jubilee frowned. "You have to know that my family isn't particularly good at talking about difficult things." She traced an invisible line on the countertop. "I'm not even allowed to talk about having cancer around my parents because it upsets them. So there are things in my siblings' lives that either we just don't talk about or that most of us don't even know about."

"That's rough."

"It is what it is. But to answer your question—I do know that something happened to Caleb his senior year of high school. You know his friend Daniel Finley died, right? In a car accident?"

Megan nodded. She'd known that Caleb and Daniel had been best friends for a long time and that Daniel's death had been difficult on everyone. Her heart clenched for Caleb's loss. Was this some kind of latent grief? Had something Megan said triggered something in Caleb in regard to the loss of his friend?

"Well, after that happened, Caleb wasn't the same. I mean, I was still a kid, but he wasn't my fun brother anymore for a while. He wouldn't talk to anyone, and he was just...angry. Then he went away to college and I barely saw him until he returned to become a police officer."

"But that's all you know?"

Jubilee smiled a sad smile. "It is. I'm sorry. I'm being totally unhelpful, aren't I?"

"No, I think you're onto something. I would just ask him, you know, if I felt like he would answer honestly."

Jubilee leaned toward her. "The thing is, is that I think out of everyone, he would tell you. He's a different person when he's around you. Seriously."

Megan's throat tightened. She could only squeeze Jubilee's hand in thanks.

WHEN CALEB DROVE by The Rise and Shine near closing time, he parked outside and waited. He'd avoided Megan for days now, except from afar. Seeing her but not talking to her, not touching her, not kissing her—it was a particular kind of torture.

He wanted to tell her about Daniel, but she'd already admitted how much she hated people just like him. How ironic. And she'd hated *him* for so long. If Caleb weren't so torn up about everything, he'd be amused at the similarities.

Around six o'clock, he waited for Megan to exit the bakery. Fifteen minutes passed, then thirty. Normally she cleaned up and walked home, but ever since she'd been followed, she drove home. He didn't see her car, though.

He did, however, see someone who seemed shifty walking down the block. Caleb's body tensed as he studied the man: he had his hands shoved into his pockets, and he kept looking around. When the man got closer to the bakery, Caleb slowly opened his car door and got out. He waited. The man looked inside the bakery, and Caleb was about to approach him when the man shook his head and began walking again.

Caleb waited. The man didn't return. He let out a breath and removed his hand from his gun. *It was just some random guy*. Probably had wanted to get something to eat but hadn't realized when The Rise and Shine closed.

But anxiety still clawed at him. Without thinking, he went to the bakery's door and, finding it locked, pounded on the glass.

When Megan didn't come to the door, he pulled out his phone to call her. The police officer in him was glad she wasn't answering the door alone, while the man in him was irritated that she wasn't going to let him inside so easily.

Before he could call her, though, she came to the door. Seeing him, she put her hands on her hips and glared.

"What do you want?" she called through the glass. "We're closed."

"I need to talk to you." It was the only explanation he could come up with at the moment.

She rolled her eyes, but finally, she unlocked the door and opened it. She didn't say anything when he stepped inside, but instead she waited, her expression impatient.

He locked the door. Even though he wore his police uniform and was wearing a gun, he still felt like Megan was the one with the gun. The metaphorical gun. Then again, he'd done this to himself, hadn't he?

He didn't think. He just said, "I've missed you."

Her expression softened ever so slightly, but she didn't budge. "So you finally read my texts? Did your phone break or are you just an asshole?"

"I'm sorry. I should've called. It's just—" He ran his fingers through his hair. "I'm an idiot. I wanted to see you. Are you okay? Why are you still here?"

"Because this is my business."

"You never stay this late."

She opened her mouth to argue, but then she rolled her eyes. "I'm doing inventory. Which I need to finish, so, yeah. I'm going to go do that."

Turning, she stalked to the back, and Caleb couldn't stop himself from drinking in her figure from behind. He let out a sigh, especially since he knew he'd be following her. No matter how hard he tried, he could never avoid the connection he felt for this woman.

Stepping into the kitchen, he saw bags of ingredients on the counters. Megan grabbed her tablet, inputting numbers with a small frown. When she saw him, she didn't react. She merely continued to work.

Caleb didn't mind the silence. He let her work, and he wandered through the kitchen, not looking for anything in particular. When he found some leftover muffins in a sack, he opened it and pilfered one for himself.

Megan said, "Those aren't for you—"

He bit into the muffin, grinning.

"God, you're annoying. Go stand over there so you don't distract me."

He did as she said, but only because he had no intention of *not* distracting her very shortly. His conscience told him he should leave her alone, but he didn't feel like paying attention to his conscience right that second. He'd missed her: the way her hair fell about her shoulders in auburn waves, or how when she bent over, he received a flash of creamy cleavage that went straight to his groin. How she fiddled with her necklace when she was thinking, or how she'd painted her fingernails a bright pink with red tips.

He finished his muffin and waited.

She tapped something into her tablet before moving to where Caleb stood. She didn't say anything, but merely brushed past him. Or she tried to. The counter blocked her from moving past him without touching him, and he wasn't about to let her go without touching her.

He snaked an arm around her waist, holding her in place. He exulted in her indrawn breath, and he trailed his fingers across her belly to her breasts. Her nipples were already tight little buds. He couldn't stop the groan from bursting from his throat.

But Megan wasn't about to surrender that easily. She pushed his arm aside and glared at him. When she crossed her arms and tapped her foot, he almost grinned.

"What do you want, Caleb?" she finally asked in exasperation.

He didn't touch her. Not this time. But he didn't need to. His gaze heated, he murmured, "I want you. I keep dreaming about you. The pillow that you slept on? It doesn't smell like you anymore. I want to see your beautiful body again, bared only to me. Taste your wetness on my tongue again. Hear the way you say my name when I plunge inside you. But mostly, I want *you*."

She opened her mouth to respond—and then she just shook her head and turned away. "I don't have time for this."

Clearly he was going to have to try a little harder to earn her forgiveness. Maneuvering around the counter, he blocked her once again from getting around him. "Megan," he cajoled. "Megan, Megan, Megan."

"Great, you know my name." She patted his chest. "Bonus points if you can spell it. There's no 'h' in there, by the way. People love to add an 'h' and I have no idea why."

"Megan Genevieve," he drawled, "you're gorgeous."

Her eyes widened a little. "How do you know my middle name?" He was about to respond, but she rolled her eyes. "Wait, never mind. You're a cop. You can probably find my second-grade report card if you wanted to. By the way, the reason I only got a Satisfactory in 'being kind to others' was because Jeff Sanderson stole my brownie at lunch and I kicked him in the shin for it."

Caleb's smile widened at Megan's babbling. He reached out to touch her, but she darted away. The slight smile on her face gave him hope.

She moved so the counter was between them, and to his immense annoyance and amusement, she leaned down on the counter so he could get a very nice eyeful of her cleavage.

"You just going to stand there, Officer?"

He raised an eyebrow. "You sure you want to taunt a guy with a gun?"

"Which gun? You seemed to have two on you today, or you're just really happy to see me."

When he growled and tried to capture her, she laughed

and slipped from his grasp. They played like that for some minutes, with Megan darting away and Caleb chasing. He almost caught her multiple times, but she somehow managed to wiggle free. Or maybe he just liked feeling her wiggle against him too much to stop.

Finally, he cornered her in the pantry. A dim light bulb provided only a small measure of light, and he could almost imagine they were the only two people in the entire world. Leaning his arm against a shelf above her head, he murmured, "I've caught you."

Her eyes gleamed as she trailed her fingers down his chest before cupping the impressive bulge in his pants. He grunted. "I think I've caught something, too." She stroked him, and Caleb's eyes almost rolled back inside his head.

"You're playing with fire."

"Maybe I want to get burned."

He tangled his fingers in her hair and was about to kiss her when she asked, "But answer one question first."

He stilled.

"Is there something you need to tell me?" Her voice was soft, hopeful, yet apprehensive. The playful look in her eyes disappeared.

He struggled. His lungs seemed like they couldn't inhale enough air. Fear coalesced inside him until it was like a living creature, tangling itself within him. He couldn't think, and he couldn't admit to himself that the possible loss of Megan from his life did something to him that was utterly terrifying.

He pushed his conscience down, down, down. Before he kissed her, he replied, "No. There isn't anything."

CHAPTER FIFTEEN

Megan wanted to believe him, but when he wouldn't look her in the eye as he said it, somewhere deep inside she didn't believe him. It hurt. It hurt, and yet, when he kissed her, she didn't push him away.

He was her ultimate weakness. *I love a man with terrible secrets,* she thought, feeling like she could cry at any moment.

Caleb was relentless, and as he took her in his arms, she almost forgot everything. She almost forgot the feeling that the ground was shifting beneath them and if she didn't watch herself, she'd get caught and wouldn't be able to emerge as a whole person again.

"I missed you." His lips roved across her cheeks, her nose, until he kissed down her throat. His breaths came in desperate pants, and it mirrored her own desire.

She tangled her hands in his hair, and she gripped the strands so tightly that he winced a little. It was an unspoken thing—*if you hurt me, I can hurt you*—and he seemed to acknowledge it with a tiny nod.

"Don't lie to me, Caleb." She licked at his bottom lip. "Because I don't forgive that easily."

"Noted," he said before nipping at her bottom lip. His hands trailed down her sides until he gripped her waist, like he was afraid she'd run away from him again.

If she were wise, she would run away. But at the moment, the last thing she wanted to be was wise. Pulling his head down, she kissed him, and he groaned when her tongue slicked inside his mouth.

They exploded together. They kissed each other desperately, like they couldn't get close enough. As Caleb roved his hands down Megan's body to grip her ass, she touched him as well, loving the feeling of his muscles underneath his uniform. When her fingers got too close to the gun in his holster, he laughed against her mouth.

"Probably should take that off." He unhooked his belt and pulled the holster off, setting it on a box nearby. "As long as you promise not to shoot me."

"If you keep talking and not touching me, I might."

He grinned and lifted her up, carrying her from the pantry out into the kitchen. Pushing bags of ingredients off of the counter, where they landed on the floor with a loud crash, he set her up on the counter. Now they were the same height. Megan opened her legs so he could step between them, and the feeling of his hardness against her already sensitive core made her shiver.

Caleb ripped open her shirt, and buttons pinged around them. Megan let out a nervous giggle. She'd never had a guy so desperate for her he literally ripped her shirt open, but Caleb seemed almost crazed with need for her. He latched his mouth onto one nipple through the lace of her bra, and the wet and the heat sent frissons of pleasure through her.

Reaching behind her back, she unhooked her bra. Caleb's eyes gleamed as her breasts came into view, swollen and begging for his touch and his mouth. He bit down on her right nipple—not enough to hurt, but enough that she felt the nip down to her toes—and she grabbed his hair. His tongue laved and his teeth bit, and when he sucked one nipple with intense pressure, Megan almost came out of her skin.

But she didn't want him to be the only one in control. Pushing him away, she began to unbutton his shirt.

"See, this is how you unbutton a shirt," she said with a laugh. "You don't have to rip it open, you know."

"Tease me at your own risk," he warned, but she only laughed again.

She pulled at his undershirt, and then he was bare-chested. His chest was scattered with dark chest hair. She traced the lines of his abdominals with a pleasured sigh. Swirling a finger around his belly button, she drank him in, loving how he trembled as she touched him. When she licked one of his flat nipples, he groaned.

She avoided the obvious bulge in his pants, only because she wanted to torment him. She nipped at his collarbone before sucking on that spot, leaving a mark that she knew would be there for a while.

"Did you just give me a hickey?" he asked in amusement.

"Yes, and if you don't behave, I'll give you another one in a spot more noticeable." She licked down his sternum, his heart pounding under her mouth. "You smell so good."

"I sprayed an entire bottle of AXE body spray on before I left."

At that, she bit his pectoral. He yelped. And then she hopped down from the counter and kneeled in front of him, her hands busy on his belt buckle.

"Megan..." he warned. "You're playing with fire."

"You keep saying that, and yet I have a hard time really caring." She delved inside his pants and boxers to enclose her hand around his hardened length. The skin was silky soft around a cock as hard as granite, and she leaned forward to lick the pearl of moisture that had formed at the tip.

He swore, but he didn't tell her to stop. His hands clenched at his sides, and she had a feeling he was barely keeping himself from having her take him entirely into her mouth.

With a coy smile, she did just that. He was too big to take to the very root, but she relaxed her throat until his tip hit the back of it. He touched her hair, almost reverently, as she sucked him and moved her mouth up and down his length. His cock glistened with the moisture, and to her delight, he only grew harder. Larger. Her body tingled as she took him deeper and faster, cupping his balls in her other hand.

"Fuck, Megan. *Fuck.*"

She knew he was close. Letting him free of her mouth, she licked the sensitive underside, her gaze glued to Caleb's.

He muttered something before pulling her up to meet his kiss. His cock bobbed between them, and he pressed it against her soft belly. With quick movements, he undid her jeans and cupped her mound through the thin fabric of her panties. She knew she was drenched already. Only a few touches would set her off.

But she didn't want to come without him, and he gave her a look that said the same. Moving her onto the counter again, he yanked her jeans and panties off of her, her shoes clattering to the floor along with her clothes. The counter was cool underneath her ass, but she barely registered the temperature. She was on fire for Caleb, and a blush had covered her from her breasts to her ears.

He kicked her legs apart so he could step inside them. They both groaned when his cock touched the sodden curls of her sex, and when he took hold of his length and began to rub her sex, she started quivering uncontrollably. He brushed her clit with the tip, and then he barely entered her. He kept doing that, over and over, and she dug her fingernails into his shoulders in desperation.

He kissed her shoulder before taking hold of her hips so he could enter her fully. Inch by inch, he possessed her, until he was inside her to the hilt. Her clit brushed against his pelvis, and she tipped her head back from the sheer sensation.

That was when Caleb cursed and tried to pull out. When she looked at him, he said, "Condom. I don't have one."

Her brain was slow to process this. Condom. That was something they needed. He didn't have one. She didn't have one, because who kept condoms at a bakery? Why did they need one? Oh, right.

Reality tried to intrude, but she pushed it aside. "Just pull out," she said.

"You sure?"

She undulated against him. "Totally, completely sure."

"Thank God." A second later, he started plunging inside her, and she squealed in delight. The feeling of his bare cock inside her couldn't compare, and she wondered why they hadn't done this before. Her brain tried to say there was a reason, but she couldn't find it. She didn't want to find it.

She just wanted him to keep filling her, his strokes relentless. He leaned his forehead against hers, and their breaths puffed together as he went faster. Megan moved with him; his fingers dug harder into her upper thighs, using that as leverage to go faster, harder.

"Come for me, baby, God, come for me." His voice was pleading. He pressed her clit with his thumb as he filled her. The sensation of his cock stretching her, his thumb on her sensitive bundle of nerves, collided together. She shattered.

Her back bowed as she came, and shivers racked her frame. She barely heard Caleb swear before he pulled out. She watched as he came on her belly, and it was the most erotic sight she'd seen in ages: Caleb losing control like this, his face contorted, his body shaking with pleasure.

Seeing him like this only made her orgasm lengthen, and she reached down to rub her clit one last time. Another burst of pleasure filled her. Caleb said her name as he kissed her, and she came with his tongue in her mouth, his seed on her stomach, and both of their hands touching her clit.

"I love you," she said suddenly. She hadn't intended to say it, and especially not naked on her bakery's kitchen counter. But it had fallen from her tongue, like she couldn't stop herself. And it felt right.

Caleb looked at her, like he couldn't believe she'd said that. His eyes were dark green pools, and Megan was afraid she'd gone too far. When he cupped her cheek in his hand, though, and he kissed her with such tenderness that her heart ached, she knew he felt the same. Even if the words were still unsaid.

Yet as he pulled away, she couldn't help but think that his kiss tasted of endings. Like he knew this would never happen again. She clutched his shoulders and he let her, but after a few moments, he pulled away. She felt like a part of herself had been separated from her very body.

"I should go." He got dressed.

Megan didn't move. Her body was replete, but her mind was racing. And to make things worse, she couldn't find her voice.

When he kissed her one last time and then helped her get dressed, escorting her from the bakery to her car, she couldn't speak. It was like someone had stolen her voice, like she'd uttered the last words she'd ever say.

"Goodbye, Megan." Caleb touched her face, and before she could say anything, he'd gotten into his car and driven away.

CHAPTER SIXTEEN

Megan couldn't sleep, and she couldn't eat. She couldn't do anything except agonize over Caleb. Jubilee's admission about Caleb losing his best friend Daniel kept coming back to her.

Something in her gut told her that Caleb was hiding something, and it had to do with Daniel. Had Caleb been there that night somehow? But wouldn't that be common knowledge?

Early on a Sunday morning, hours before she'd have to go the bakery, Megan sat at her computer and stared at the screen. Her heart pounded in her chest. It would be so simple to Google what she wanted to know. Assuming Google could even tell her. If no one in Fair Haven had so much as whispered about Caleb's involvement in Daniel's death, she doubted it would come up on Google like when you searched for purses or a highly rated plumber.

What if you find out something you don't want to know? That was the real conundrum. Because Caleb could only be keeping something from her that he truly didn't want her to know.

But she couldn't let the whispers go. She typed in her search terms, and the first hit was an old newspaper article almost fifteen years old.

Fair Haven High School Student Dies in Late-Night Crash

She scanned the article and winced at the photograph of the mangled car at the top. *Daniel Finley, 17 years old of Fair Haven, Wa., was driving on Daughtry Road early Saturday morning on March 23. At approximately 3:32 AM, his car crashed into a tree. Finley was killed on impact. Toxicology reports are pending. The funeral will be held on March 30 at First Hill Presbyterian Church, with family and close friends attending a private ceremony later in the afternoon.*

She didn't see anything about Caleb as she read the rest of the article that described Daniel as a top student and talented athlete. Peering at the photo of the mangled car, she looked for some evidence of Caleb, but there was nothing. Of course there wasn't. Did she think she was some kind of Sherlock Holmes?

She let out a tense breath. Her heart ached for Daniel's family, and she couldn't help but compare this accident to her own arrest. She'd been fortunate that she hadn't driven to the party she'd attended, otherwise she wasn't sure she wouldn't have been stupid enough to have gotten behind the wheel.

But she wouldn't give up quite yet. She continued to search, finding any bits and pieces she could pull up. Nothing gave her the clues she'd wanted. She once again returned to the photo of the mangled car, and something set off alarm bells in her brain.

The car had been T-boned when it hit the tree. She'd known that already. But as she peered more closely, she saw that it wasn't the driver's side that had been smashed like a child's toy. It was the passenger's side. But Daniel had been driving—hadn't he?

Her breath caught in her throat. It wasn't improbable that Daniel would've been seriously injured regardless, but her gut told her otherwise. She began searching for more images, hoping against hope there was something somewhere that would show her the driver's side of the car. Finally, she found it on a blog that hadn't been updated in years, a rather macabre website of some of the state's worst car accidents. She shuddered at the pages and pages of smashed cars before finding Daniel's car.

This photo allowed her to see the driver's side. She wasn't surprised to see that the driver's side looked like the car hadn't even been hit.

Daniel had to have been the car's passenger. And she knew, without even hearing him say it, that Caleb had been the driver.

Megan called Sara. When Sara heard the emotion in Megan's voice, she said, "I'll be right there."

Megan unlocked the front door and sat down with Gary on her lap. Gary, though, didn't appreciate Megan's overly rough petting, and he jumped down from her lap to sit on a chair by himself.

"What's going on?" Sara asked as she came inside. She looked like she'd just gotten out of bed, and her hair was in a messy ponytail.

Megan wondered if her sister had come from Harrison's place, which only made her think about Caleb.

Her heart twisted. And before she could stop herself, she burst into tears.

Sara instantly went to her and pulled her into a hug, like

she would do when Megan was little. Burrowing into her sister's embrace, Megan cried until her eyes hurt, and she was sure she didn't have any tears left. Her heart broke into so many pieces she knew she wouldn't be able to put them all back together again. She cried for Daniel, for Caleb, for herself. She cried for the pain and guilt of adolescent mistakes that ended in such tragedy.

Sara didn't ask her what had happened. She held her close, stroking her hair, and those simple actions allowed Megan to calm herself enough to explain what was going on.

"Is it Caleb?" Sara asked. Her expression brimmed with concern. "Did you two break up? Have a fight?"

Megan shook her head. "It's worse than that." She lowered her voice to a whisper, "I think he's keeping something from me. Something awful."

"Like what? What are you thinking?"

Megan wiped at her face and after getting her laptop, she showed Sara what she'd figured out only hours earlier. Sara furrowed her brow as Megan tried to explain.

"So you think Caleb was the one driving that night? Is that it?" Sara frowned. "But how could that be? Wouldn't they have reported that?"

"I thought the same, but I just keep feeling like there's something else that happened. I asked him more than once, but he wouldn't say anything."

"Doesn't that confirm it then? That nothing happened?" Sara rubbed Megan's shoulder. "Because Caleb doesn't seem like the type of guy to do something like that. I know you two haven't always been on the best of terms, but just consider the logistics. There's no way this could've been kept hidden for this long, right?"

Megan wanted to believe her sister. She hoped against hope that she was seeing something there that didn't exist, but it didn't help with her anxiety. She needed to talk to Caleb, otherwise she would be a basket case for the rest of the day.

"If Caleb was drinking and driving and his friend died..." Megan rubbed her eyes, despair leaking into her voice. "I don't even know. It's too much to think about. And on top of it, he lied to me about it?" Her bottom lip trembled as she said it out loud.

"Don't let yourself get worked up until you know the truth, okay? Do you want me to go with you? Do you want me to talk to Harrison? If anyone knows the truth, it would be him." At that statement, her eyes darkened. "And if he does know, then he's been keeping secrets from me, the jerk."

Megan smiled a little at that. Sara had always protected her, and she knew her sister would do so for the rest of her life. "No, but thank you. And don't be too hard on Harrison—it wasn't his secret to tell, if it's actually true." Megan looked away, her heart aching, yet also full of love for her sister. And for Caleb, despite everything. "I never deserved a sister like you, you know."

A slight blush bloomed on Sara's cheeks. "What are you talking about? I did what I had to do. For us. It wasn't a matter of anyone deserving anything."

"I know, but you took on the brunt of it. I hid behind you, and I knew I didn't need to. And then I got arrested..." Her voice trailed away, memories flooding her mind. "I repaid you by doing something stupid. I'm sorry."

"Have you felt guilty about this for this long?" Sara asked incredulously. "Megan, you did something stupid, yes, but you were young. We all make stupid, thoughtless mistakes in our lives. Yes, even me. It's how we repair those relationships and work to earn the forgiveness of whomever we've hurt that matters most."

Megan closed her eyes. Who had she hurt the most? Caleb. And now he was hurting her.

Would they ever manage not to hurt each other, or would this be the vicious cycle they'd trapped themselves in?

"Go talk to Caleb," Sara urged. "Right now. He's probably not even on duty today. Go. You need to know the truth, and sitting here with me isn't going to get you that."

Megan hugged Sara tightly, letting herself be the little girl who could rely on her sister for just a moment. Then she pulled away and knew that she had to face reality—and adulthood—even if it resulted in breaking her own heart.

CALEB WASN'T surprised when Megan showed up on his doorstep early on Sunday. The look in her eyes explained it all. Terror and anger and guilt overflowed in equal measures.

The moment she stepped inside, she asked, "Were you there the night Daniel died?"

This is it. This is the end. Suddenly, it wasn't terror he felt—it was an infinite sadness. Sadness because he'd dug his own grave, and there was no one to keep him from suffocating.

"Yes, I was," he replied.

Her mouth tightened. "Were you the one driving? Not Daniel?"

"Yes. It was me."

They stared at each other. Megan struggled to breathe, and when she seemed like she was about to collapse, Caleb went to catch her. But she lurched away like she couldn't bear his touch.

"Don't. I can't. You *lied* to me, and about something like this." She backed away, shaking her head. "You were drunk that night, weren't you? And so was Daniel. You got behind the wheel, and somehow, you survived."

"You've got it exactly," he said, his voice dull. "How did you figure it out?"

"I saw the photo of the car. So it's really true? That's it?"

"Yes."

She covered her mouth with her hand, and there was such pain etched onto her face that Caleb felt like his heart was going to splinter right then and there. He'd never hated himself as much as he did in that moment.

"I'm sorry." His voice was gruff, toneless. "I should've told you, but I thought once you knew, you would hate me." The laugh that burst from him surprised them both. "And look? I was right. You hate me."

"It's not...it's not that simple. I trusted you, yet you wouldn't tell me the truth. That's what's breaking my heart right now, along with what you did. My heart breaks for Daniel, and even for you. I can't imagine the guilt you've shouldered for so long." Her voice cracked.

Caleb ran his fingers through his hair, disheveling it. He couldn't stop his agitated movements—a muscle in his jaw ticked, and a headache roared in his temples.

"I can't believe after everything I told you, about my mom, about you arresting me for *drinking*," Megan said incredulously. "I spilled my heart to you, but you couldn't do the same? What does that say about how you feel about me?"

He wasn't a good man. He was a fraud, and a coward, and

he should've left Megan alone. He knew that. But if he was sure of anything, it was how he felt about her.

He took her by her upper arms, holding her captive. "What does it say about how I feel about you?" he whispered, hoarse. "It says that I'm so in love with you that I couldn't bear the thought of you leaving me and even worse, hating me. That I love you so much it's physically painful." His fingers dug into her arms. "I can't sleep, I can't eat. I can't *live* because you are the one person who gives me a reason to keep going. It's always been you. Haven't you realized that yet?"

Her eyes glimmered with tears. "But you still lied to me."

He stepped away. "Yes, I lied to you. Do you know that I've lived with the guilt of that night for close to fifteen years? That my own parents covered it all up to make it look like Daniel had been the one driving? They bribed everyone in this godforsaken town and I was a coward and didn't try to stop them. I thought maybe they could make it go away." His breaths were coming in puffs, and he couldn't get enough air. He felt like the walls were closing in on him. He buried his face in his hands, but it didn't stop the memories.

"Caleb..." Megan breathed. She placed a hand on his forearm.

"Don't touch me." He lurched away, and when he looked at her, he knew, *he knew*, it was over. "Don't look at me with pity. I don't deserve it. I killed my best friend and I let my parents cover it up because I was terrified."

She didn't speak. Only her tears spoke to him, spilling from her eyes to shimmer on her cheeks.

He had to explain—even if it didn't make one bit of difference. "Do you know why I became a cop? Because I thought maybe, I could work for the rest of my life to right my wrongs. But it doesn't work like that, does it? It doesn't bring Daniel back from the dead. I've tried to abide by the letter of the law without fail, and I've served this community because I needed to show to myself that I could do something good for once."

Megan just cried harder. "Oh, Caleb. You were both drinking that night, weren't you? You were young, and stupid, and I know what that's like. Don't you think out of everyone, I would understand that? When you're that age, you're so sure you're an adult, but you're just a kid. A kid trying to act like nothing in life can hurt you. I *get* it. I would've at least tried to understand if you would've told me." She wiped the tears from her cheeks, but they kept coming. "But how can I trust you now with this between us? You didn't think I was someone worth confiding in. Were you planning on never saying anything at all?"

"No," he said fiercely. "I wanted to tell you. But how could I when you'd told me how much you hated drinkers? I couldn't, Megan. I couldn't tell you without losing you in the process."

"Don't you see, though?" Her voice was barely a whisper. "You've already lost me. You lied about something so huge…" She swallowed. "I can't stand being lied to. Not about something as big as this. How do I even know who you are? I feel like I've never really known you."

Caleb was shaking, and his heart rattled against his ribs. He felt like the rope he'd grabbed onto was slipping from his grasp.

In one last move of desperation, he hauled her into his arms. He couldn't let her go—she was his heart, his very soul.

She was everything, and he was nothing. "I love you. Doesn't that mean something?"

"It means everything." She cried harder, and he couldn't stand it. He couldn't stand to see her shedding tears over him.

He kissed her, tasting the salt on her lips, and she sobbed against his mouth. They kissed until he was sure their bodies had melded together. It was a kiss that spoke with so many emotions that he shook from it. He tasted her love and her despair, and he wanted to take all of those emotions into himself.

Megan broke away. "I can't do this. I can't. I'm sorry."

When she left him finally, he didn't try to stop her.

CHAPTER SEVENTEEN

Caleb stared at his glass of whiskey, watching the light create shimmers of color in the liquid. He hadn't yet drunk a drop of it, and as he sat at the bar of the Fainting Goat, he knew he wouldn't take a sip.

He pushed the alcohol away, disgusted with himself.

It had been a week since he and Megan had ended things. He hadn't spoken to her, and the few glimpses he'd gotten of her had ended with her avoiding his gaze. He'd stood outside her bakery more than once, about to go inside and get her to take him back, but he couldn't do it.

He was a coward, as always.

"You look like shit," a voice said behind him. Harrison sat next to him and motioned to the bartender. "I'll have your darkest beer," he said.

Caleb glowered at his older brother. He really was not in the mood for whatever it was Harrison thought he needed to say. So he decided to act like Harrison wasn't there.

Too bad his brother could never catch a hint.

"Sara told me some of what happened," Harrison said

finally. "I'm assuming that's why you look like you've been kicked in the balls twenty times over. Also, she's pissed at me for keeping secrets from her, even though I told her they weren't *my* secrets." He looked annoyed. "So, thanks for that."

"Since you already know what happened between me and Megan, why are you here asking me about it?"

"Don't bite my head off. I told Sara that you needed time alone, but she insisted that I was being a stupid man." He sipped his beer, considering. "I think it's time that you finally forgive yourself, Caleb."

The rush of guilt filled Caleb until he couldn't breathe. It had been like this ever since Megan had confronted him, and it was almost impossible to find his balance again. The woman he loved hated his guts, and he deserved her disgust. What could he do? Go back in time and change the past?

"I don't deserve forgiveness. Not for what I did to Daniel, and not for lying to Megan."

"Do you know what I think?"

"No, but I'm sure you'll tell me anyway."

"I think, to you, forgiveness means you'll have to confront what happened and, yes, what you did. Because otherwise, you can push everything aside and try to act like nothing ever happened."

Caleb leveled a look at his brother, anger eclipsing any other feeling right now. "What the hell do you know? Why is it that everyone else knows what I should do? You weren't there. You think I'm acting like nothing happened? Fuck you." His head spun. He was in that car, trapped, seeing Daniel's mangled body next to him. The blood running down his friend's face; the smell of it, metallic and bitter. The sound of him calling out Daniel's name until his voice was hoarse.

Caleb put his head in his hands. The bar and his brother disappeared, and in that moment, he was back in that car. He wanted to scream until his voice gave out.

"Hey, buddy. Look at me. Caleb, look at me."

Caleb looked at Harrison. His brother seemed out of focus, and the room began to spin dangerously.

"Caleb, you're not there. You're in the Fainting Goat with me, your brother. The brother you think is a giant pain in the ass."

Caleb blinked. "You're all a giant pain in my ass."

"True, but since I'm your only older brother, I like to think I get the top spot." Harrison waved to the bartender again and pushed a glass of water in Caleb's direction. "Drink something. And don't complain, otherwise I'm going to pull physician's rights and take your ass to the ER."

Caleb gulped the glass of water, its coolness clearing the dizziness from his head. Wiping his mouth, he muttered, "You're a pediatrician."

"Pediatric oncologist. Now, are you going to faint on me or not?"

Caleb gave him the finger, which seemed to reassure Harrison enough that he wasn't in danger of keeling over.

"I don't know how I can forgive myself." He felt exhaustion swamp his body. He hadn't slept in days. How could he, when one dream was about Megan, and the next was about Daniel? Even worse, sometimes the dreams twisted together, and it wasn't Daniel dead in that passenger seat—it was Megan.

"I don't know, but you need to. I never agreed with our parents covering this all up. I know they thought they were protecting you, but we both know they were afraid just as much for our family's image as they were for your future." Harrison let out a breath. "I really shouldn't have been surprised to see how Mom acted when I started dating Sara."

Caleb grunted.

"Whatever happens, though, I'm here for you. We all are. We love you, and we want you to be happy."

His head swimming and his emotions in turmoil, Caleb could only nod. He hadn't realized how much he needed to hear someone say those very words, but they opened something in his soul. Perhaps it was the first piece of absolution he needed.

And as he sat with Harrison, neither of them needing to say a word, he knew what he had to do next.

When Caleb saw the small woman with gray-streaked hair sitting in the coffee shop, he felt like a teenage boy again. He hadn't seen Stephanie Finley since Daniel's death, and although she'd aged, she had somehow remained the handsome woman he remembered.

He walked up to her table and, not sure what to say, waited for her to notice him.

"Caleb!" Stephanie rose and enveloped him a tight hug. "Oh my word, look at you! You're so tall. And wearing that uniform? Sit, sit. How are you?"

Caleb had played over and over in his mind how this encounter would go after he'd replied to Stephanie's email. He'd expected, at the very least, a cold reception from her, if not outright antagonism. He'd practiced his apology more times than he could count, and he'd envisioned all manner of things. Stephanie yelling at him, throwing her drink in his face, crying.

But not this. Not this genuine kindness and, unless he was losing his mind, joy at seeing him.

"I'm good," he said huskily. He had to force his hands underneath the table to hide their shaking. "You just moved back here?"

"That's right. Oh, I'm so glad you decided to see me." She reached into her purse to grab a tissue, dabbing at her eyes. "Seeing you just brings everything back, you know? You were like a second son to me."

He wanted to crumple at her feet. He wanted to beg her to forgive him. Yet the only words that emerged were: "I'm sorry. For everything." He coughed to cover the feeling of impending tears. "I should never have let my parents cover up what happened. I should've been charged and gone to jail for what I'd done, but I was a coward then. I'm still a coward, but I want you to know that I'm not keeping this a secret anymore. I can't bring Daniel back, but I can clear his name. Since I was formally charged with a lesser crime, I can't be charged with what I deserved now, but I can find a way. Something. I got off too easily."

He didn't know what else to say or how to go on. He grabbed his glass of water and gulped it. The sound of the glass hitting the table seemed to echo through the café.

Stephanie regarded him with sad eyes. Finally, she covered his hand with her own. "Can I be honest with you?" After he nodded, she said quietly, "When Daniel died, I wanted to blame someone. I wanted to blame *you*. You got behind that wheel when you knew you shouldn't have, and in those early days, I wanted to scream at you. I wanted to ask why you had survived and my son didn't. I blamed you with every fiber of my being, and I blamed your parents, and God. Everyone. I wanted to hate you."

Caleb's heart squeezed until it hurt. "I don't blame you."

"But then I saw you after the funeral, and I realized that the situation could've been reversed so easily. Both of you were drinking that night. Daniel had driven you two there, and I would bet that he'd been drinking before that, right?" At Caleb's silence, she nodded. "I'm not saying you shouldn't feel guilty, or that everything was all right after that. I struggled. I was in a dark, dark place, but after the years passed, I began to remember my son as my son. Not as my child who died that night."

"How can I ever make up for what I did to you?" Caleb whispered. "I don't deserve forgiveness."

"Maybe not, but I'm going to give it anyway." She squeezed his hand. "I forgive you, Caleb. If you loved Daniel —and I know you did—you'll live your life to its fullest and not stay in the past. You made a stupid mistake because you were young and you thought you were invincible. But what does your guilt do for Daniel? It won't bring him back."

"I should've been charged, though. How can you say that? I got off without a scratch. I got to live while Daniel..." He swallowed against the lump in his throat. "It wasn't fair."

"Perhaps, but I think you've suffered for years in silence, haven't you? I can see in your face that's the case. I can't imagine a worse punishment than never-ending, silent guilt." She let go of his hand, but her eyes remained as kind as ever. "I moved away because this place had too many memories, but I returned to care for my mother. When I realized you lived here, too, I knew I should see you, because I want you to know that although you hurt me, and Daniel, and others, that doesn't mean you don't deserve forgiveness. So here it is again: I forgive you."

Caleb's shoulders slumped, and he covered his face with his hands. When Stephanie moved her chair to sit next to him, rubbing his shoulder, he didn't stop her. He might not deserve her words, but he drank them in like rain after a drought. The chains around his heart loosened, and for the first time in what felt like an eternity, he saw the light at the end of the long, dark tunnel.

"Thank you," he murmured.

She passed him a tissue from her purse. "Don't thank me. Just show me—and Daniel—that you're going to be the man we both knew you were going to be. Promise me that."

He could—and would—promise just that. She gave him a watery smile, and he brushed tears from his cheeks.

After they talked of the past, and of Daniel, and the happier times, Stephanie said, "I was going to visit Daniel today. Would you like to join me?"

Caleb almost said no. He shouldn't be there, but Stephanie's insistence allowed him to accept.

They drove to cemetery in silence. The sun was out today, bright and shining, and when they reached Daniel's head-stone, Caleb saw that colorful flowers had been planted around it. His breath caught when he read the inscription—*Daniel Jonathan Finley, Born May 11, 1984, Died March 23, 2002. Beloved son. May your soul rest in angels' arms*—he couldn't speak. The sun felt too hot on his shoulders, and he was afraid he'd collapse right there.

He'd never visited Daniel's grave. He'd avoided it because

he had never felt like he had a right to say goodbye. The tears fell, endless rivers, and Stephanie took his arm.

"I'm so sorry," Caleb could only say, over and over again. "I'm so sorry, Danny. It should've been me, not you."

Stephanie was silent, tears in her eyes, and Caleb found the strength to kneel in front of his best friend's grave. He traced his fingers over the inscription.

"You should've been the one to live, but the universe has a wicked sense of humor, doesn't it?" He wiped his eyes. "I'll live my life for you, and I won't hide what I did any longer. The truth deserves to be set free. I hope you can forgive me. God knows I can barely forgive myself."

When Stephanie laid a hand on his shoulder, he covered it with his own. They stayed just like that, whispering the words they wanted Daniel to hear, and slowly the wounds of old began to heal.

When they parted, Stephanie giving Caleb a big hug, he felt hope for the first time since the accident.

"Be happy, Caleb," she murmured. "Be happy, if not for yourself, then for Daniel. He would've wanted that."

"I will. I'll do it for him, and for you." He hugged her one last time when they returned to the coffee shop. "If you need anything at all, don't hesitate to let me know."

"Of course. The same goes for you." Before she got into her car, she said, "Oh, and Caleb? Don't let happiness slip from your fingers, not when you get so close to it. I know more than most that you have to fight for that happiness."

He couldn't speak; he just nodded.

As he watched Stephanie drive away, he knew what he needed to do.

<h1 style="text-align:center">CHAPTER EIGHTEEN</h1>

Caleb drove straight to Megan's house. He felt free, his heart unburdened, and it was like a revelation. He might not be worthy of Stephanie's kindness, but that didn't mean he wouldn't clutch it to his heart as hard as he could. And now he knew that he had to get Megan back. Without her, he was only a shell of a man.

As Caleb drove up to Megan's house, though, he felt a chill crawl up his spine. The initial excitement of seeing her faded to cold terror. After so many years on the force, he'd come to rely on his instincts, and his instincts were telling him that something wasn't right.

Caleb wasn't on duty, but he still carried his gun. Parking his car a block away, he quietly walked to Megan's house, taking in the surrounding houses and yards. He didn't see anything. It was early evening, and the streetlights had only just turned on. But that feeling—the indescribable feeling of doom—had latched its fangs into him. He hurried his steps. *If anything happens to her...*

Fear wanted to eclipse everything. The thought of Megan

getting hurt was almost too much to bear. He couldn't let fear overwhelm him—he had to stay on alert. Eyes wide open and capable. Any amount of panic could result in tragedy.

He walked the perimeter of her house. He almost believed he'd been paranoid for no reason, until he reached the back door. Broken glass littered the porch, and the door hung wide open. He pulled out his gun.

That was when he heard her scream.

It was a sound that he would never, ever forget.

"I need backup immediately," he said after calling the station.

"Roger that, what's the situation?"

"Break in with homeowner inside. I have reason to believe this is the same perpetrator who robbed Megan Flannigan's bakery. I'm going in now."

"Backup is on its way."

He maneuvered around the door, creeping into Megan's house. After that initial scream, silence had fallen. He strained to listen, to find where this creep was, and he heard shuffling. It was coming from her bedroom. Panic almost closed his throat, but he had years of training that kept him calm.

He stepped as silently as he could, trying not to crush any more broken glass into the carpet. He heard a thump. Slowly rounding the corner, he made visual contact, confirming that both the perp and Megan were in her bedroom. The light was just enough to show him that the man had his hands on Megan, and red covered his vision.

He burst through the open doorway. "Police! Drop your hands or I'll shoot!" he roared, his gun pointed straight at the man.

The man hauled Megan against him, and she gasped.

Caleb barely restrained himself from killing this guy. He wanted to rip out his throat like some kind of savage animal. When he saw the stark fear on Megan's face, his rage only worsened.

"Drop your hands and let the woman go!" When he didn't move, Caleb's voice rose. "Either step away or I'll shoot you where you stand!"

Caleb couldn't see any fear in those eyes. If anything, the man seemed almost amused, like this were some kind of elaborate game. He wasn't wearing a mask this time, either. When Caleb saw the scar on his lip, he knew without a doubt this was their guy.

The man finally put up his hands, letting Megan go. She hurried to Caleb's side.

"Get out of here," Caleb told her, never letting the man out of his sight. "More officers are on their way."

Megan wouldn't move. She was clearly in shock, her face pale and her eyes wide, and Caleb wasn't sure she'd even heard him.

Caleb couldn't help Megan with the threat of this criminal still very present. Pressing his gun to the man's back, Caleb began to check him for weapons. He pulled out the guy's wallet, and he finally was able to ID him: Jason Worth of Seattle, Washington.

"You done yet?" Jason sneered. "I have places to be."

"Shut your mouth. Turn around, now."

Jason obeyed, although his mouth and scar still stretched in a grim smile as Caleb moved to finish checking him for weapons.

Megan still hadn't moved, to Caleb's infinite frustration. "Megan, get out of here," he commanded. "*Now.*"

She finally seemed to come back to herself. She opened her mouth to speak, and it was enough distraction for Caleb to give Jason the small opening he'd needed.

With a flick of his wrist, Jason pulled a wickedly sharp knife from his jacket, slashing at Caleb's face. Caleb fell to the floor, and Megan screamed.

"Caleb, he has a gun!" she cried.

Jason smiled at her words, right as he pulled a gun that he'd managed to hide in his jacket. "And look at that? The girl was right. She's smarter than you'd think." Although he initially pointed the gun at Caleb, he slowly swiveled so the gun pointed at Megan.

Caleb slowly rose from the floor, his own gun pointed at Jason, his forehead stinging from Jason's knife.

"I wouldn't move, if I were you," Jason said to Megan although his gaze stayed on Caleb. "Otherwise I'll blow your brains out. That would piss you off, wouldn't it, police boy? I've seen how you keep following this one around like some kind of stray dog."

Caleb inhaled a deep breath. Frissons of fear ran through his body, but his grip on his gun was steady. One false move could be the end of the woman he loved. "What do you want?"

Jason shrugged. "What else? Money. I tried getting it from this bitch's stupid bakery, but she didn't have anything really worth stealing. And then you guys decided to follow me, and, well, I thought I'd have a little fun before you caught me. Maybe enjoy something first." The man sneered. "I've seen how you all look at her. She got a magical pussy or something?"

"Shut your mouth, you piece of shit. Either put down your

gun, or I'll shoot." When Jason didn't move, Caleb shouted, "Put down your gun, now!"

The moment slowed to a standstill in Caleb's mind. He saw Jason unlatch the safety of his gun—a swift movement of his fingers—and he knew a second before it happened that he was going to shoot Megan. Caleb fired. Jason fired as well. Something hot hit Caleb's shoulder at the same time that Jason went down, screaming, clutching his belly.

Caleb gasped for air. Agony filled his entire body. He sank to the ground, and he couldn't figure out what was going on. He realized that Megan had her hands on his shoulder as he looked up at her. She kept saying something. She had blood on her hands. Why were her hands bleeding?

"You idiot! Dammit, Caleb Thornton, if you die on me, I'll find you in the afterlife and haunt you for all eternity!"

Caleb didn't understand what she was talking about until she pressed his shoulder. White-hot pain lanced through him. He cried out; it was like a hot poker had been shoved through into his skin.

He vaguely heard the sirens and saw the beams of light. He barely noticed when backup arrived, shouting orders and taking control of the situation. He only knew he had to tell Megan what she meant to him, because if he died with her hating him, he'd be trapped in his own type of purgatory.

"I'm sorry." He gasped for breath. He babbled. "I'm so sorry, baby. I shouldn't have lied to you." He winced when she pressed harder on his wound.

Her face shone with tears, and she looked fierce as she said, "Shut up. Just shut up. It doesn't matter, because you're going to survive this and we're going to be happy. Nothing else matters." Tears fell from her eyes and dripped down her chin, landing on his face. "I love you, you idiotic, impossible man."

That was when he heard someone else say his name, and then he was being placed on a stretcher and taken out to an ambulance. He called Megan's name. She climbed into the ambulance, and after she took his hand, he let the blackness take him completely.

CHAPTER NINETEEN

Caleb realized two things when he opened his eyes: one, that he felt like shit, and two, he really needed to pee. After a few more moments, he finally figured out that he was in a hospital. Why was he in a hospital? And hooked up to a machine?

He glanced down at the IV in his arm, and his brain was sluggish in processing this information. What the hell was wrong with him? He touched the IV, which resulted in a flurry of activity at his side.

"Don't you dare pull that out," a nurse warned, although he saw a smile on her face. She looked familiar. He'd seen her before at the bakery.

The bakery. Megan. *Megan.* The man in her bedroom. Bullets. Blood. He gasped.

He tried to sit up, but he was too loopy to manage it. He grunted something and was about to demand this woman tell him where Megan was when Megan herself appeared at his side.

Megan smiled down at him, her red hair like an auburn

halo around her. Her face was drawn and she looked pale, but she seemed all right.

"Thank God," she breathed as she leaned toward him. "You're awake."

"How long have I been out?" His voice was croaky and rough.

"For twelve hours or so. They had to take you into surgery to remove the bullet from your shoulder. It just barely nicked an artery." Her face paled further. "It was a really close call."

He closed his eyes. He was exhausted. The small part of his mind that remained lucid told him it was from the painkillers, currently being fed into his arm via that IV.

"What happened? Are you all right?" He drank her in, and his heart started beating so quickly that the machine next to him started beeping more loudly.

The nurse came by to rest a hand on his shoulder. "Take a deep breath for me, Caleb. That's it. One more for me. There you go." The nurse looked at Megan. "Be sure to keep him as calm as you can, okay? I'll give you two some time alone, but call me if you need anything."

Megan nodded as the nurse exited. She took Caleb's hands as she sat down next to him, squeezing his fingers.

"You almost died, you jerk," she said, tears making her voice husky. "You jumped in front of a bullet for me, and for a minute there I thought I'd lost you." She struggled to gather her composure.

He reached out to touch the tendrils of hair near her cheek, and she leaned into his touch. She sighed deeply.

"What about the shooter? Where is he?" His face flushed with anger when he remembered Jason Worth's smirk.

"He's alive, barely. You shot him in the stomach. If he

lives, he'll be charged with so many crimes there's no way he's getting out of jail anytime soon. Not to mention that assaulting a police officer is kind of a big deal, you know."

She lifted his hand to her cheek and kissed his fingers.

Caleb knew he needed to say something. To tell Megan something important. His thoughts kept jumping around, and he could barely hang onto one before it slipped from his grasp. Megan seemed to sense his struggle and made soothing noises.

"It's all right. I know. You just need to get better."

He shook his head. Groaning, he sat up a little bit. "I need to say this." He looked into her eyes, bright blue and clear as a summer sky. "I'm sorry for lying to you. I shouldn't have done it. I was so scared that when you found out about Daniel that you'd hate me, but lying to you only made that worse. I don't blame you if you do hate me. I get it. But I won't let you go, Megan. I love you. I love you so much—"

She stopped him with a kiss. His heart exulted, and he kissed her with everything that was overflowing within him. When his vitals started to spike again, though, she pulled away with a reluctant smile.

"I know. I love you, too. I shouldn't have pushed you away like that. Yes, you lied to me, but how could I judge you for a mistake like that when I did the same thing?"

"Nobody died because of you." His voice was haunted.

She touched the white sheet on his bed. "Yes, but the only reason I wasn't in your shoes was sheer luck." Her lips tilted upward, but it was a sad smile. "And because somebody arrested me before I could make the same mistake. When you were lying on my bedroom floor, bleeding? You saved me, Caleb. You've always saved me, even when I didn't deserve it.

You're not only the man that I love: you're the man who's made me into the woman I am today."

He shook his head, because he didn't deserve those words. But Megan—if he knew anything about her—was relentless. Relentless in her ambitions and relentless in her love. Like the afternoon in the cemetery with Stephanie, peace once again washed over him.

Maybe he didn't deserve forgiveness—whatever that meant. But that didn't mean he shouldn't take it when it was offered in all its humbling glory.

"I talked to Daniel's mom," he said quietly. "She told me I should forgive myself."

"And she's right. You were young, Caleb. That's not to say you didn't do something that hurt a lot of people, but living in guilt for the rest of your life won't bring Daniel back."

He let out a deep breath. Closing his eyes, he imagined his future, and for the first time, it involved only happiness. Love. Joy. A woman who'd saved him just as much as he'd saved her.

"But if you jump in front of another bullet," Megan warned as the painkillers threatened to put him to sleep once again, "I'll kill you myself."

He just smiled as sleep claimed him.

When Caleb awoke again later that afternoon, Megan decided that she couldn't very well keep his family away from him, even if she wanted him all to herself.

"You're okay with everyone coming in to see you?" she asked Caleb for the millionth time.

"If all else fails I'll fake a heart attack," he joked. Megan gave him a dirty look and vowed revenge for that remark when he was better.

The entire Thornton clan—Dave, Lisa, Mark, Harrison and Jubilee—along with Sara, James, Ruth, and a number of Caleb's fellow police officers, including Officer Gonzalez, had been sitting in the waiting room for hours now. When Lisa had heard the news, she'd driven straight to the hospital to demand to see her son, even though he'd been in surgery. She'd then questioned all of the doctors and nurses like she worked for the CIA. Finally, Dave had taken her arm and made her sit down, which resulted in her bursting into tears.

Megan's heart swelled when she saw the plethora of people waiting for news. Although Megan wasn't family, she'd been brought in the ambulance with Caleb, and as such, had used that to her advantage. She felt a little pinch of guilt when she saw the stark, white faces looking at her for an update on his condition.

"He's awake again," she said. "He's still loopy from the meds, but he said he wants to see you all."

James hopped up from his chair, about to run to see his soon-to-be uncle, but Sara took him by the arm before he could scamper away.

"I want to see him!" he complained. "We've been waiting *forever*!"

"We will in a minute," Sara replied. "Should we go in groups?"

Right then, Abby Davison, who'd been attending Caleb and had been a steadfast presence for all of them, came inside the room.

"Let's do groups of two or three first, all right? We don't

want to overwhelm him. His recovery looks good, but he lost a lot of blood."

Megan couldn't help but notice the way Mark seemed to glower even more when Abby was around. If she weren't so wrapped up in Caleb, she'd investigate that story as soon as she could.

Dave and Lisa saw Caleb first, and Megan sat with Sara during that reunion. Sara took Megan's hand and squeezed it, smiling at her and giving her strength. Megan was so tired that she could collapse right there on the floor.

"Why don't you go home?" Sara murmured. "You need to shower. Eat something. Get some sleep."

Megan shook her head. "I can't leave yet. Not until he's out of the woods completely." Her throat closed, and she couldn't stop herself from remembering what it had been like seeing him bleeding onto her bedroom floor, his eyes glazing over. How he'd told her he'd loved her like he'd been afraid he'd never get the chance again. How he'd been rushed into surgery and nobody could tell her his outcome until hours later.

She swallowed against the imminent tears. She was tired of crying. Mostly, she wanted to go to Jason Worth's hospital bed and kick him in the head. According to Officer Gonzalez, Jason had been committing petty crimes for years but, due to financial trouble, had decided to up the ante. Megan's bakery had merely been one of his multiple targets. When robbing her bakery hadn't proven fruitful, Jason had decided to take out his frustration on Megan.

Or so Jason had told the police. Megan only cared inasmuch that he would be sent to jail and never be free again. Not just for hurting her, but for almost killing Caleb.

"He's going to be all right," Sara said in a firm voice. "The outlook looks good, and he's young and strong. Besides, he has you to live for."

Harrison leaned over Sara's shoulder to add, "He also knows that he has five siblings who will haunt him if he so much as thinks about dying."

That made Megan laugh, although it was a watery one. Megan then noticed that Ruth sat a little distance away, and guilt assailed Megan, seeing her mother there but not part of the group. Tired of the anger and the grief, Megan went to Ruth and said quietly, "Come sit with us."

Ruth looked up, surprised. She hesitated, but at Sara's nod and Megan's insistence, she sat closer, no longer separate from her daughters.

Jubilee sat down next to Megan and put her arm around her while James tried to entertain everyone with his impressions. James only knew that his uncle had gotten hurt, but he didn't know the extent of it. As a result, he was the one bright spot in a room of very gloomy adults.

"Aunt Megan, are you and Uncle Caleb getting married?" James asked in a loud whisper. "I heard my mom say that you were."

"James, I did not say—"

"Yes, you did. Two days ago." Harrison smiled wider at Sara's dark look.

Sara just crossed her arms, although her mouth twitched in a smile.

Megan looked at her nephew, and her heart filled with love. Enfolding him in a hug, she replied, "I don't know if we are, but if we do get married, you can be in the wedding. How about that?"

James hooted in triumph, which caused both his mother and his almost-stepfather to shush him before they got yelled at by hospital staff.

Dave and Lisa emerged after thirty minutes, Lisa dabbing her eyes with a tissue. Megan couldn't help but feel sorry for Lisa: she'd lived her life fearing what other people would think of her if they discovered that she—and her children—were human.

To Megan's surprise, Lisa approached her. She felt Sara stiffen next to her, and she could only imagine the look on Harrison's face.

"You were with Caleb when he was shot?" Lisa asked.

Megan nodded. "He took a bullet meant for me." Her throat closed around those words, and she found that she couldn't say anything else.

"That's just like my boy." She gave Megan a veiled look. "If he could have, he would've told the world what really happened. The concealment was at my insistence." She looked pale and wan, and Dave put his hands on her shoulders. "It's one of the things I regret most in my life."

She then looked at Sara and Harrison. Megan held her breath. "I'm sorry for what I did. Truly sorry. I'm not sure there's a way to make up for it, but if I can, I'll do my best."

Harrison and Sara stared. No one moved, and the tension in the room was palpable. Jubilee tightened her arm around Megan.

Finally, Sara stood and took Lisa's hand. Her expression wasn't friendly, but it was open. Accepting. "Thank you," was all she said.

Harrison rose next to his fiancée. "I'll walk you two out."

James, still on the floor, turned his wide-eyed gaze to Megan when the trio left. "What was that lady talking about?"

Megan opened her mouth to answer, but Abby came into the room right then. Mark, who'd been sitting by himself, suddenly looked up at Abby's entrance.

Abby, for her part, had yet to acknowledge Mark at all. Her gaze was solely on the group with Megan. "You can come in now."

Megan followed Sara, James, and Mark; Harrison would be joining them shortly. Ruth had said she preferred to stay in the waiting room, as she wasn't family. Although Megan wanted to argue that point, Sara had shaken her head. "One thing at a time," Sara said.

Caleb looked tired, with dark circles under his eyes, but when he saw Megan, he lit up. When she reached his bedside, he took her arm and pulled her down for a kiss that was so deep that Megan was bright red and almost panting when it ended.

Sara gave them both a wry look, while James looked disgusted. "Why are you kissing her like that? Gross!"

"Adults kiss like that," Mark said in a low voice. "Someday you might even like it."

Everyone was so astonished by Mark speaking that silence reigned for a few moments.

"Maybe he won't like it, though. You don't know what he'll like when he's an adult," Abby countered. She had her hands on her hips, her brow furrowed.

Everyone else waited in silence, their gazes darting between Mark and Abby like they were watching a tennis match.

Mark's lips thinned. "What, do *you* not like kissing?"

"That's none of your business." Abby's voice was prim. She moved to grab a chart next to Caleb's bed, and Megan saw that her cheeks were pink.

"Maybe you just haven't been kissed by the right man," was Mark's rejoinder.

Megan looked at Caleb. He gave her an "I'll tell you later" look.

Abby and Mark seemed to have forgotten that anyone else was in the room. Megan didn't know how to break the silence, but luckily, her nephew did.

"Kissing is gross. I don't think I'll ever like it." He climbed up onto Caleb's bed and asked, "Aunt Megan says she isn't sure if you guys are getting married. Do you know if you're getting married?"

Sara looked like she wanted to muzzle her child, but Caleb surprised everyone by saying, "I haven't asked her yet, but I will soon. I hope she says yes."

His gaze was only on her when he said those words. Her heart thrilling, she leaned down to kiss him for a second time. But that resulted in James making disgusted noises again, and everyone laughed. By the time the kiss had ended, Abby had left the room, and Mark had returned to his usual taciturn state.

Megan snuggled against Caleb as the group chattered; even Mark spoke more than once in his gruff way. When Caleb took her hand and enclosed it in his, she knew nothing could compare to the love and happiness she felt at this moment.

EPILOGUE

Megan couldn't help but smile when she heard the booted footsteps behind her. Continuing to knead her dough, she acted nonchalant when solid arms wrapped around her waist.

"Whatcha making?" Caleb asked. "Cinnamon rolls?"

"Bingo." When he kissed her neck, she giggled. "I can't work when you do that!"

"Then stop working and help me out."

"What's your problem now?"

He pressed his burgeoning erection against her ass, and in revenge, she wiggled. He groaned.

"You aren't making my problem any better, you know."

She laughed. Turning in his arms, she reached to cup his face, but then she saw the flour on her hands. She narrowed her eyes, and when he figured out her intention, he ducked from her embrace.

"Don't you dare—!" He pivoted, but he wasn't fast enough.

With a laugh, she planted her floured hands on his freshly

washed uniform, leaving bright white handprints right over his pectorals.

He growled like a baited bear. "You'll pay for that."

"Oh, no, how awful. What're you gonna do? Spank me?"

His nostrils flared. "Don't tempt me."

When he grabbed her and was about to toss her over his shoulder to have his evil way with her, Megan didn't remotely resist. She looped her still floured hands around his neck as he carried her toward the pantry. But since the universe liked a good joke, Jubilee came into the kitchen a moment later.

"What are you two—oh geez, not this again. Get a room. Go rent one of the rooms next door and go there. Don't sully the bakery with your shenanigans."

Caleb glared at his sister. "You could always leave, you know."

"Too late. Megan, we're out of vanilla syrup. Do we have any in the back?"

Megan climbed down from Caleb's arms, now in business mode. She saw him give his sister another dirty look, which only amused her further.

"I think we have another bottle..." She searched and finally found the offending bottle, handing it to Jubilee. "Here you go. Has the rush started? I'm almost done with these cinnamon rolls."

"Not yet, so you two have a little time to do something indecent. Just don't be too loud, okay?"

"Jubi..." Caleb warned, but she only laughed and scampered out of the kitchen.

"She's right, you know," Megan mused. "We do need a room."

"We have lots of rooms. I distinctly remember using this one in particular."

She poked him. "No, I mean, a room we…share." At his look, color climbed up her cheeks, and she instantly felt foolish. She could've mentioned that question not quite so awkwardly.

His green gaze darkened, and even with floured handprints on his chest, he managed to be the sexiest thing Megan had ever seen. After the shooting and his surgery, he'd recovered with remarkable speed, probably because he hated being cossetted and had wanted to return to work as soon as possible.

Although his doctor had advised that he take it easy, he'd returned to the force within a month's time. Officer Gonzalez had insisted on desk duty for another month, however, and she knew Caleb was itching to get back to real police work.

Her heart hurt when she thought of him bleeding out on her bedroom floor and waiting in the hospital to hear if he'd made it. Every time she saw the scar on his shoulder, she couldn't help but feel a flare of hatred for the man who'd put it there. Jason Worth remained in jail without bond after recovering from his own injuries, and he would go on trial for multiple felonies within the next few months. Everyone was relieved that Jason was off the streets and behind bars for the time being.

Two months later, she and Caleb still lived in their separate houses, although more often than not he would end up at her house in the evenings. He told her it was because he liked her place better, but she had a feeling he'd formed an attachment to Gary and just wouldn't admit it.

Caleb had also begun to come to terms with Daniel's

death. He'd finally started the process of forgiving himself, and although it would be a difficult journey, Megan knew he would make it through the guilt and pain. Megan filled with pride every day that he worked on himself, which also gave her the courage to do similarly.

She'd finally met with Ruth and been honest with her. They would never be the best of friends, but Megan knew she couldn't shut out her mother for the rest of her life. They both needed to heal, and Megan couldn't stay angry any longer. Life was too short to hold onto that kind of bitterness.

The Thornton clan—including Lisa Thornton, to everyone's surprise—had welcomed Megan. Lisa would never be a warm mother-in-law by any means—baking cookies and offering to babysit future grandchildren—but Megan considered it a boon that she had finally decided to let her children live their lives.

Well, at least for the time being.

Megan and Caleb had only fallen further in love with each other. Every day somehow eclipsed the one before it. Their nights—and days—were filled with passion, and every hour with love. Megan never knew her heart could be as full as it was now. How had she ever thought she could live without this man?

Now, Caleb assessed her. "What exactly are you saying?"

She turned to finish rolling out her dough. "I'm saying that it seems silly to live in two separate houses when we see each other almost every day. It would be more economical to combine incomes—"

He turned her toward him. "You want to move in together?"

She couldn't gauge his reaction, and it sent a flurry of

panic through her. Maybe he didn't want to live with her? Or he thought it was too soon? She scrambled for a reply, but he spoke first.

"I'll move in with you, on one condition."

She blinked. "What?"

"That you marry me first."

Her world shifted on its axis, but in the best possible way. For so many years she never thought she'd find a man she'd fall in love with, let alone marry and live together for the rest of her life. But she knew this was right—not just right, but perfect.

She smiled so wide that her cheeks ached. "Are you proposing?" she couldn't help but tease.

For the first time, he seemed unsure. Rubbing the back of his neck, he muttered, "I had planned on doing it the usual way, but you surprised me."

"Well, then, I'll wait until you have everything put together. I can't say yes to a sort-of proposal. And where's my ring? I can't be a fiancée without a ring on my finger."

His lips twitched. And then, before she could react, he dipped his hands into the bag of flour on the counter and smeared it down her arms and chest.

"You jerk!" she cried out, laughing so hard she couldn't breathe. "Is this how you propose to a woman? You're terrible at it!"

Yanking her into his arms, he touched his nose to hers. "Yeah, but you love me anyway, right?"

"I guess I do." She sighed.

He nipped at her mouth, and when he kissed her, she knew without a doubt that regardless of Caleb's proposal skills, they would live happily ever after—covered in flour or not.

When Abby Davison, resident nurse at Fair Haven Memorial, looked at the chart handed to her by the physician on call, she couldn't stop the annoyed hiss escaping from her mouth.

Mark Thornton.

Of course he was here. Of course he had a broken arm and—surprise!—she would be the nurse attending him.

She couldn't help but wonder what would happen if she told Dr. Smythe she couldn't attend this patient. *Sorry, Doc, but he's a Grade-A asshole who insulted me for no reason and I'm still mad about it. His arm can stay broken for all I care.*

Yeah, that would totally work.

Abby had known her fair share of asshole men. Her ex Derek had been one of them. When he'd broken up with her because she wasn't the image of feminine beauty he'd wanted—also known as skinny and blonde with fake boobs—he'd done a number on her self-esteem. Abby had never been what anyone would call skinny, and although she'd gotten to a point that she'd not minded her curves, her ex had destroyed any good self-image she'd managed to create.

After her break-up, she'd given up on men. Men only hurt you, and she didn't have time for that kind of BS. She had her job, which she loved, and she had her friends and family.

She winced when she thought of her family, that same family that asked her every time they saw her when she was going to find a man and get married. As if that was the pinnacle of a woman's achievement in life. Had her mother skipped Feminism 101? Apparently so.

Within the past month, her mother had become relentless, setting her up on dates with men that were not even remotely her type. The type of men who texted their mothers at the table, or who gave her detailed accounts of their various surgeries when they found out she was a nurse. Abby was to the point of being so desperate to avoid another one of her mother's dating schemes that she'd signed up for online dating just to find a random guy she could present as her boyfriend to give herself a breather.

It was a terrible idea, of course, but desperation tended to breed terrible ideas.

When she'd first seen Mark Thornton, though, she had to admit to herself that he was handsome: darkly handsome, in a mysterious kind of way. He was clearly the black sheep of the family. What had made him separate himself from them like that? She knew Lisa Thornton was a force to be reckoned with, but her other children hadn't distanced themselves like Mark apparently had.

Of course, she was basing this off of seeing him only a handful of times. But after years as a nurse and working with a variety of people, Abby had discovered that first impressions generally gave a fairly accurate picture of people.

And her first impression of Mark? Surly. Rude. Thoughtless. He'd insulted her and called her a "mousy nurse."

What an asshole. She was glad she had had the courage to call him an asshole to his face. She had a feeling very few people ever did.

But Abby had never been the type of person to hold onto grudges for too long, and she knew that allowing Mark to know his words had affected her would only give him some kind of twisted enjoyment. She put on a calm, professional smile as she entered his hospital room

"Mr. Thornton," she said, "it looks like your arm is broken. I'll be the nurse putting on your cast. I'll go over aftercare and help you set up follow-up appointments. You'll have the cast removed within two months, as long as the break seems to be setting well."

Mark, in all his handsome glory, scowled mightily from his hospital bed. He looked like he'd been run over by a tractor, although according to his chart, he'd been thrown from his horse. She wondered why he'd come all the way to Fair Haven when he lived an hour away, but apparently he'd broken his arm last night and, after driving up to Fair Haven, had only just decided to get his arm looked at.

Typical male.

"Is a cast really necessary?"

His voice made the hairs on her arms stand on end, and it sent a pleasant shiver through her body. *Yes, he's handsome. Remember, he's also a total jerk.*

"It is, unless you want the break to heal at a weird angle, thus making it difficult, if not impossible, to use your arm like you would've previously. Or, even worse, we would have to re-break your arm and reset it, which I can assure you, is not a nice process."

He glowered, but he finally grunted in agreement. Gathering the necessary items, Abby set to work, and although Mark wasn't a chatty patient by any means, he wasn't a difficult one. Even when she knew he was in pain—his face drawn and his forehead beaded with sweat—he didn't once complain. She'd had men twice his size burst into tears when she'd reset their bones, but not Mark.

Impressed despite herself, she couldn't help but go a little easier on him after she'd finished placing the cast on his arm.

"I'll have Dr. Smythe give you a prescription for Vicodin that you can take as often as needed, although don't operate heavy machinery or drink while taking it. It can make you sleepy, so I always caution patients to start with a small dose."

"I don't need it," he said as he moved to stand up from the bed. At her surprised look, he added, "Painkillers make me sick. I have to get back to work, and I can't be falling asleep while wrangling my horses." His tone was irritated, like she was wasting his time while trying to do her job.

Any sympathy she had for him melted away like ice under a hot lamp. "Well, you don't have to take it, but I'll get you the script just in case," she said primly. She made a note on his chart. "Let me go get Dr. Smythe."

"Wait."

She turned, raising an eyebrow. *What is it now?*

"Look, I don't know what you have against me—"

Now her eyebrows practically disappeared into her hairline.

"But whatever it is, can we just let bygones be bygones?"

She opened her mouth to reply, but she was so stunned by not only his lack of apology but his placing the blame squarely on *her* that she couldn't think of anything to say.

He seemed to sense her disquiet because he shifted uncomfortably. She had to admit he looked rather pathetic, his arm in a huge cast, his face pale and covered in stubble. He winced when he tried to stand.

The nurse in her couldn't let a patient hurt himself, even if she disliked that patient as a person.

"Don't try to stand yet," she advised before helping him to sit down again. "You've been through a fairly traumatic injury, and getting a cast set is painful. Don't push yourself too hard or you'll only extend your recovery."

He practically growled when she touched him, almost rearing back. "I don't need your help," he snapped.

She rather wished she could shove his head into a bucket, but she gritted her teeth and kept her cool as she assisted him back onto the bed. And to her intense annoyance, she couldn't help but notice the coiled strength in his torso and how he smelled like horses and sweat. What would it be like to have a man like this take you into his arms? Kiss you until you saw stars?

As their gazes caught, he seemed to sense the same electricity between them. Her hand was placed near his heart, and it thumped beneath her palm. His eyes darkened—a green so dark they seemed black—and she saw that although his face was hard and his jaw was like iron, his lips were well-formed. Soft.

Maybe you just haven't been kissed by the right man yet. His words echoed in her mind.

She almost jolted away, but she forced herself to help him onto the bed. She practically jumped away from him once she saw that he was settled.

Confused and ill at ease, she muttered, "I'll get the doctor now," before she hurried from the room.

❧

MARK KNEW he'd fucked up. Seriously fucked up, and he didn't know how to make it better. He'd pissed off the pretty nurse, and he only made things worse every time she came near him.

Why did she have to be the one to see him like this? Grumpy, in pain, and off his game?

He grumbled, punching the pillow behind him. He waited for Abby to return like a good patient, but after almost fifteen minutes had passed, his patience waned. He didn't even need those damn painkillers. Rising from the bed with a pained grunt, he gathered his things and was about to leave his room when he heard Abby's voice in the hallway.

"Mom, I don't have time for this right now. I'm at work."

"How else can I talk to you? You never answer my calls or texts. It's like I don't exist!" The woman's voice was shrill, and Mark winced at the sound.

"I'm sorry. I'm just busy." Abby's voice was cajoling, although she also sounded annoyed. "I need to go, okay? I'll call you tonight."

"I'm here because I set you up with a great date—no, don't give me that face, he's a podiatrist from Bellingham and he's an amazing catch—"

Mark's ears perked. Abby's mother was setting her up on dates? He had a hard time imagining her needing help to find a man. For all he knew, she had scores of men lining up to touch that gorgeous body, those full lips, those creamy breasts...

"Mom, no. I told you no more dates."

"But you're twenty-eight! When will you finally settle down, Abby? When you're fifty? I'll be dead by then. I'll never get to meet my grandkids!"

Mark rolled his eyes, and he could imagine Abby doing the same.

But then his eyes only widened when he heard Abby's next statement:

"You don't need to set me up on a date because I've met a guy. We've just started going out."

Her mother gasped. "Who is it? Do I know him?"

"No, but you know his family." After a beat of hesitation, Abby said as clear as day, "His name is Mark Thornton."

ABOUT THE AUTHOR

A coffee addict and cat lover, Iris Morland writes sexy and funny contemporary romances. If she's not reading or writing, she enjoys binging on Netflix shows and cooking something delicious.

www.ingramcontent.com/pod-product-compliance
Lightning Source LLC
Chambersburg PA
CBHW050359190726
48284CB00007BB/2353